THE BUMP IN THE BOSS'S RETURN

SCARLETT CLARKE

ROMANCE

If you purchased this book without a cover you should be aware that this book is stolen property. It was reported as "unsold and destroyed" to the publisher, and neither the author nor the publisher has received any payment for this "stripped book."

Recycling programs for this product may not exist in your area.

ISBN-13: 978-1-335-21704-2

The Bump in the Boss's Return

For questions and comments about the quality of this book, please contact us at CustomerService@Harlequin.com.

Harlequin Enterprises ULC
22 Adelaide St. West, 41st Floor
Toronto, Ontario M5H 4E3, Canada
www.Harlequin.com

HarperCollins Publishers
Macken House, 39/40 Mayor Street Uppe
Dublin 1, D01 C9W8, Ireland
www.HarperCollins.com

Printed in U.S.A.

1 2 3 4 5 6 7 8 9 10 HDC 28 27 26 25

Scarlett Clarke's interest in romance can be traced back to her love of Nancy Drew books, when she tried to solve the mysteries of her favorite detective while rereading the romantic chapters with Ned Nickerson. She's thrilled to now be writing romances of her own. Scarlett lives in, and loves, her hometown of Kansas City. By day she works in public relations and wrangles two toddlers, two cats and a dog. By night she writes romance and tries to steal a few moments with her firefighter hubby.

Also by Scarlett Clarke

Harlequin Romance

Royal Encounters

The Prince She Kissed in Paris
Royally Forbidden to the Boss

Summer Escapes

The Billionaire She Loves to Hate

How to Inherit a Fortune

Snowbound Nights with Her Best Friend

Visit the Author Profile page at Harlequin.com.

John and Mom,
another romance across the finish line thanks to you.

To my readers,
thank you for making this dream possible for me.

How to Inherit a Fortune

Step one: get married!

Long-lost cousins Arlowe, Mina and Ivy have all received a first-class ticket to Salzburg—and an invitation to the will reading of the grandmother they've never met. Shock doesn't even begin to cover it! Until they're told...

...they have just a year to wed!

If they don't make it to the altar before the twelve months are up, they'll lose out on their share of a million-dollar inheritance.

All three women have more questions than they do answers. And with so much at stake, dare they risk adding their hearts in the mix as well...?

Read Arlowe's story in
Snowbound Nights with Her Best Friend

Read Mina's story in
The Bump in the Boss's Return

Both available now!

And look out for Ivy's story,
coming soon!

Dear Reader,

I'm excited to bring you this second installment of How to Inherit a Fortune, a trilogy about three cousins who could inherit millions...if they find husbands within a year! Ireland is still on my travel wishlist, but researching the country was truly a treat. Róisín by the Cliffs, the castle-turned-hotel where my heroine Mina works, was inspired by real castles like Dromoland Castle. Weaving in historic details like the Brehon Laws and the centuries of falconry helped me bring the eastern coast of this beautiful country to life.

I also loved diving into Mina's character. Like so many of us, she wants to let go of pain from her past and move forward, yet can't help but look back. As I wrote, I realized it wasn't about closing the door on her pain. It was about learning to live with it, to embrace the good days and reach out for help on the challenging days. A truth Barrett realizes for himself, too, as he works on fully embracing how he feels about Mina. The resulting relationship between her and Barrett, one where they can both be vulnerable and support each other, is the love story Mina deserves.

Scarlett

CHAPTER ONE

Mina

THE WAVE CRESTED, white froth churning at the peak, before the water slammed into the cliff-side. Mina Callahan watched the familiar battle between sea and limestone from a hundred feet above as her fingers gently caressed the swell of her stomach.

One day.

She smiled slightly. One day she would bring her son or daughter here to *Eascarraig*, the Waterfall Rock. Watch the newborn lambs, in the spring, chase each other among the bright yellow gorse blossoms. Picnic on the emerald hills in the summer and early autumn. Collect blackberries and wild mushrooms as the weather cooled and water poured over the cliffs into the ocean.

A gust of wind burst over the edge of the cliff and barreled toward her, tugging at her cloak and whipping her curls about her face. She closed her eyes and breathed in the salty scent of the sea as she pressed her hand tighter against her belly.

Something pressed back—a hand, perhaps, or even the heel of a tiny foot.

Tears pricked her eyes. Her baby would be coming around New Year's. She hadn't realized she was pregnant until nearly eight weeks along. She'd used the last five months to get used to the idea of becoming a mother, to prepare to be a solo parent the way her own mother had. She had made so many plans.

And now Barrett Sawyer, her ex-boss and father of her child, was coming to Glenvarra.

Except she hadn't told him about the baby. She'd started countless letters, picked up the phone a dozen times to call or text. But the stinging echo of his final words always stopped her.

You betrayed me. Betrayed this company.

Dismissed because of a simple Georgian town house. Number 18, Ellison Square, Mayfair. One of hundreds of holdings of Sawyer Development. When Barrett had included the town house in a list of properties to be demolished and rebuilt during a routine meeting, she'd asked why. The estimates for renovating versus demolishing and rebuilding had been negligible, less than fifteen-thousand pounds. But he'd simply told her it was his decision, and that was final.

So, she'd done her job. Written up her concerns, along with a summary of Westminster's conservation policies, her apprehensions about increased scrutiny of Sawyer Development should it become known they'd demolished a locally designated historic property, and an alternative proposal. Submitted it to the risk and compliance officer.

She'd never imagined she would stop by Barrett's office later that same day. Had never dreamed she'd spend the night in his arms.

And had certainly never thought her report would be fast-tracked to the board and voted on the morning after her night with Barrett. A vote that would pick her proposal over his.

He'd called her to his office after the board meeting. The fury in his voice had been unmistakable, so at odds with the cool, detached boss she'd crossed swords with at every turn. Completely unlike the man who turned her knees to jelly every time he said her full name, Sabrina, in that deep, husky voice. The man who, just the night before, had kissed her like he'd die if he didn't touch her.

Before she had overcome her shock at his outburst and explained why she'd argued against his acquisition, he'd told her after her internship was over, he never wanted to see her again.

Just like her father had rejected her mother when she'd told him she was pregnant.

Another gust of wind sent chills creeping down her spine. Almost identical to the cold that had settled in her stomach when he'd apologized through gritted teeth for crossing a boundary. Used words like *mistake* and *regret* that burned shame into her skin.

For a moment, the ache returned, carved out by the memory of disgust in Barrett's eyes and her own humiliation. And then she'd mentally shut it off. The pain, the ache, all of it. Lifted her head high, told Barrett she understood, and walked out of his office without a backward glance.

Barrett had left for a conference in the States the next day, making the last two weeks of her internship a little more bearable. She'd walked away with a stellar letter of recommendation and a sizeable bonus she hadn't been able to touch. It had felt more like a payoff for keeping her mouth shut than an actual honoring of her work. Her night of passion and unexpected sweetness had been turned into a sordid, shameful lapse in judgment.

One with a consequence she hadn't anticipated.

She opened her eyes and looked down at her stomach. There was no way to hide the telltale curve of her belly. As soon as he arrived, he'd know.

Her gaze flicked back to the ocean. Even the water seemed restless today, the waves pitching up here and there in dark swells. When she went to London a year ago, she'd thought she was going on a grand adventure. She'd envisioned a year living in a big city, of finally getting to put her degrees in conservation studies and business to work. Imagined what it would be like to review historical records and architectural drawings by day and explore London at night.

She'd gotten to do some of that. In the five months she'd worked for Sawyer Development, she'd conducted on-site surveys in the town house, a Victorian warehouse, and even a Tudor-era church. She'd collaborated with an interior designer on an office building renovation and prepared a presentation for a board meeting of a well-regarded American company.

What she had not envisioned, or rather who, had been Barrett Sawyer. The CEO of Sawyer Development himself. She certainly hadn't envisioned leaving London with her heart ripped down the middle.

Breathe.

One deep breath. Release. Then another. Filling her lungs as much as she could before slowly breathing out. She'd done a lot of deep breathing the last seven months. Had reframed what had happened in London, from her ill-fated night with Barrett to the gut-wrenching aftermath of the board meeting.

At least Barrett had kept his word. What had happened in London hadn't followed her back to Ireland. She'd been welcomed back by her mother. Even when she'd started to show, the villagers had been supportive.

Gossipy, she acknowledged with a small smile, but supportive.

And there was her job. Heritage and events consultant for the renowned Róisín by the Cliffs.

She glanced over her shoulder. The castle-turned-hotel stood tall and proud just over the hill. Weathered gray stone blended with the gloom of the morning. But it still held onto its elegance, its centuries of intrigue and secrets. Turrets stabbed up to the sky. Scarlet flags emblazoned with the hotel's logo snapped and waved in the breeze.

Inside, the tapestry-covered entrance hall would be quiet after the rush of the lunch crowd. Staff would be working behind the scenes to prepare the afternoon tea served in the drawing room. Guests would be tucked away in the library or the spa, with the more adventurous vacationers seeking out the stables for a horseback ride or the mews to meet the falcons kept on-site.

Another blast of damp and chilly air raced over the edge of the cliff. Tore at her cloak, whistled in her ears as fear trickled in.

Was Barrett coming to make sure she was keeping her mouth shut? Or worse, had he found out about the baby?

I'll be in Glenvarra next week. We need to talk.

Even though she'd removed him from her phone, she'd still recognized the number. He'd only sent the one text. No follow-up, no phone call, no additional information. She'd read it and reread it until her eyes hurt from staring at the screen for so long.

How many letters had she started over the last five months since she'd found out about the baby? How many times had she picked up the phone to call or text? But every time she had, the stinging echo of his words had stopped her.

There's no reason for us to ever see each other again.

As much as she didn't want to admit it, she was scared. Scared everyone's goodwill and support would evaporate once they realized the father of her baby was her former boss. What would that do to her career?

Her stomach clenched. What would Mama say when she found out the truth? Not only had her daughter made the same mistake falling for the wrong man but had taken it one step farther and slept with her boss. Mama had been so supportive. She hadn't pushed, hadn't asked questions. She'd simply offered her love.

Just like she had weeks ago when Mina had received her invitation to the will reading for one Desdemona Gruber. Mina had known as soon as she read the name out loud that it had something to do with the father she'd never known.

Mama's face had gone white, her fingers curling into fists as she'd struggled to keep her breathing steady.

"Jakob's mother," Mama had finally whispered. "Your father."

Mina turned away from Róisín, faced the sea once more. After all these years, she finally had a name. She hadn't pressed her mother for details. But she had looked him up as soon as she'd been alone and discovered why her mother hadn't wanted to share much about Mina's father. The man had been a spoiled, selfish, greedy playboy. He'd lived hard and died in a car crash in Montenegro.

There was grief. But above all she felt regret. All those years she'd spent pining for him, wishing she could have known him. So much emotion wasted on a man who had abandoned her mother and caused countless others pain.

She'd still gone to the will reading, held at a real-life castle in Austria. And at least something good had come out of it. Her tiny family had grown by two cousins, Arlowe and Ivy. She now had twenty-five thousand euros in her bank account, and potentially fifteen million more if she followed the edict of Desdemona's will and married within the year. A ridiculous requirement, but she had a friend lined up to help her fulfill it.

She had no interest in a traditional marriage right now. Not after the disaster with Barrett, and certainly not with a baby on the way.

She hadn't liked Barrett when she'd started at Sawyer Development. Cold, overly confident, and too handsome. Always polished with his tall, leanly muscled body clad in bespoke suits, his thick brown hair brushed back from his sculpted face. He could turn on the charm when he wanted, but those occasions had been few and far between. They'd clashed almost from the beginning. He liked new things, shiny things. She was dedicated to preserving history and honoring the past.

But then had come that cool spring night. She'd blamed what had happened between them on numerous things: the late hour, the rain pattering gently on the glass, the unexpected conversation as they'd reviewed notes for the board meeting, the intimacy of sharing a meal in the dark shadows just before midnight.

Whatever had led to that first soul-shattering kiss hadn't mattered in the cold light of day.

The baby did a long, leisurely roll inside her. She wrapped a protective arm over her bump. No matter what happened, she would never regret the life growing inside her. She'd always wanted to be a mother. While she never imagined it happening this way, she would make the most of it, just as her own mother had. And while it would hurt like hell if she lost her job, she would pick up the pieces and move on.

A quick glance at her watch made her sigh. Her break was over in twenty minutes. She needed a little extra time to navigate the path back down to the Róisín.

With one last look over the sea, she turned and started down the path. Reddish-brown mud clung to her boots as a faint mist started to fall. She pulled the hood of her cloak up just before a sense of warning whispered across her.

Her head snapped up. A man was approaching. Even through the hazy mist, she knew him in an instant. The dark hair brushed back from his smooth forehead, the broad shoulders beneath a black coat with brass buttons, the determined stride as his long legs ate up the distance between them.

She froze. Part of her wanted to flee, to turn around and hope he'd dismiss her as just a random woman out for a stroll.

But that wasn't the kind of woman she was raised to be. That wasn't the kind of person she wanted her child to see, to emulate. She wanted her son or daughter to be strong, to fight even when they wanted to flee.

So, she straightened her shoulders and raised her chin as Barrett Sawyer drew closer. She didn't move when his head came up, when his ice-cold eyes met hers through the rain. She didn't flinch when his gaze dropped down to her stomach. Nor did she retreat when he looked back up at her, shock and anger rolling off him in palpable waves.

Grim resolution settled deep in her bones even as relief eased the weight of indecision from her shoulders. Whatever happened next, her secret was no longer a secret.

CHAPTER TWO

Barrett

SHE LOOKED LIKE a siren, standing there in the middle of the path with red-gold curls spilling out from the hood of her cloak. With the dark sea to her right and the misty emerald hills to her left, it wasn't hard to imagine she had magically conjured the cold rain slipping beneath Barrett's collar and trailing down his back.

When he'd first seen Sabrina standing there, had recognized it was her, there had been a jolt of sorrow, a pang of unexpected longing that tightened his lungs.

But the magic of the moment was obliterated by the sight of her rounded belly beneath the long drape of her cloak.

He blinked, shock creating a roaring in his head that competed with the rumble of the sea. He knew what he was seeing. It couldn't be his. She would have told him. Yet as his head snapped up, as he took in the cold mask of her face and the determined press of her lips, the truth hit him with the force of a battering ram.

Sabrina Callahan was carrying his child.

The roaring died down as anger started to churn inside his chest. They hadn't even said a word to each other, and already Mina was slipping past his defenses, evoking emotions he'd suppressed for years with an ease that infuriated him.

He forced himself to walk up the hill, to keep his steps measured. She was playing a game, making him come to her. Normally he would have fought to balance the scales.

But he didn't care about fairness or power. Answers were more important.

He stopped a few feet away. Despite the chaos clawing at the cage he kept his feelings in, yearning slipped through once more, a thin tendril that curled through him as Mina met his stare. Aside from the glaringly obvious swell of her stomach, she hadn't changed much. Still the same oval-shaped face and smooth cheeks, the softly rounded tip of her nose matching the delicate curve of her chin. He'd thought of her as sprightly, naive, even chirpy during the five months she'd worked for Sawyer Development.

But now her full lips were pressed into a thin line. There was no warmth in her face, no lingering sparkle. Just a brittle hardness in her blue eyes he'd never thought her capable of.

A hardness, he realized that was unsettling because of how familiar it was. The same hardness he lived his life by. Was this what everyone else saw?

"Is it mine?"

His voice came out strong, authoritative. The kind of voice that made wealthy men and women around the world flinch as they lowered their eyes.

Mina merely raised an eyebrow.

"Good morning to you, too, Mr. Sawyer. It's been a while."

"I would have been here a lot sooner," he ground out, "if you had bothered to inform me you were pregnant with my child."

Her chin tilted up. "I never said it was yours."

A different type of anger gripped him, sharp claws that pierced skin and bone as they wrapped around his chest and squeezed.

Jealousy.

It shouldn't matter that she'd been with someone else. Their night together had been a mistake. But the thought of her kissing another man, sharing herself the way she had shared herself with him, hit like a punch to the gut.

Something flickered in her eyes.

Suspicious, he took another step closer. "Is it mine, Sabrina?"

Her shoulders curved in a fraction before she turned her head and looked out over the sea. The wind ripped the hood off her head and sent her curls flying in the wind.

His breath caught. She'd almost always worn her hair up in London, wrapped into a bun on top of her head or plaited down her back. The one time he'd seen it down had been that night, when he'd run his hands through the silken strands the same color as molten fire.

"Yes. It's yours."

He stared at her profile, at the flush in her cheeks from the misty rain and cold wind, the long length of her neck he'd trailed kisses down as they'd forgotten who they were for a few blissful hours. Though they'd disagreed on a regular basis, he'd quietly appreciated her honesty. Even when he didn't agree with her thoughts, he'd always known what she was thinking.

But the woman before him now was a mystery. As was the reason why she had decided to keep the most important thing that had happened between them a secret.

His eyes dropped once more to her stomach. A baby. He was going to be a father.

He'd never once imagined himself in such a role. He knew his reputation and lived up to it. He was a cold, hard man who preferred business over personal connections. Not the best personality for maintaining loving relationships. His focus had been rewarded with financial success and a drama-free existence since he yanked the reins of Sawyer Development away from his spoiled idiot of a father.

But there was no way he'd ever let his child grow up wondering why their father wasn't around. No chance he'd ever let his son or daughter experience the hell he'd grown up in.

"How did you know I was up here?" she asked quietly.

"I didn't. Someone in town recommended the trail."

He'd wanted—no, needed—to clear his head before he saw her again. But instead of a relaxing stroll through the Irish countryside, he was staring down his pregnant ex-lover.

"Were you ever going to tell me?"

Slowly, she turned her head to look at him. Her expression didn't change as she regarded him with that cool disdain she'd pulled on so easily.

"The last time we saw each other, you said if I ever showed my face at Sawyer Development after my internship, you would ensure I never worked in my field again."

Guilt crept through the anger, settled low and heavy in his gut. He had said that, among other things, in those tense minutes after the board meeting. The one where Mina had derailed his latest project by bypassing him and submitting a report stating her concerns about his plans to demolish the town house and rebuild. A report the board had agreed with and then voted in favor of restoration.

Just the thought of the town house had him

gritting his teeth. Of all the properties, Mina had picked that one to wage her campaign. The town house his father poured thousands of pounds of company money into renovating to please his latest mistress. Renovations not only paid for illegally but done quickly and shoddily. A worker had almost died. If Barrett hadn't intervened, Sawyer Development would have paid the price in lost projects, clients, and its decades-long reputation. The townhouse represented everything Barrett hated: deceit, thievery, dissipation.

And Barrett had learned just how little his father had ever cared about him in the parlor of that townhouse. More than once, he'd wished it would just burn to the ground. Barrett didn't begrudge Mina doing her job. But to submit that report without talking to him first, like she had with everything else up until that point, and then to sleep with him hours later…

Perhaps it was simply his lot in his life to have people offer him affection with one hand and then yank it away with the other. Her betrayal hurt because he'd let her in. It hurt more than any woman had ever hurt him.

The price to pay for letting one's walls down. He had no reason to feel guilty. *None*, he told himself firmly.

"I spoke harshly," he finally said. "But surely this situation warranted at least a letter."

For a moment, the only noises were the distant roar of the waves crashing against the cliffs and the almost imperceptible hush of mist drifting across the grass.

Then Mina inhaled, a sound that rose above everything. "No. You made it clear how you felt about me. Your stances on relationships and parenthood are also well-known." Her mouth tightened. "Give me one reason why I should have told you."

"Because I had a right to know!" He ran a frustrated hand through his damp hair. "Just because I didn't think I'd have kids doesn't mean I don't want to be involved."

Uncertainty flickered on her face.

Sensing the softening of her defenses, he pressed forward. "We obviously have a few things to work through. But I won't back down from this. From you or the baby. I always fulfill my obligations."

The uncertainty evaporated. Her eyes flashed with anger as she settled a protective hand on her belly. "This isn't an *obligation*, Mr. Sawyer." Her voice still carried that rhythmic accent, yet every word was heavy with disgust. "It's not an acquisition or a merger or property. It's a baby, a child who needs love and a parent who will be present. I don't know why you came here. But if it was to hurt me or punish me further, you can't. I've moved on with my life, and you have no place in it."

She brushed past him, her steps carrying her down the path away from him.

He turned, following her sure movements despite the slick mud.

She stopped a few feet away and glanced back over her shoulder. Her frown deepened when she saw him watching her. "Go back to London, Mr. Sawyer. There's nothing here for you."

He watched as she maneuvered down the hill. Every instinct screamed at him to go after her, to fight, to demand answers and not let her go until they settled everything.

But he possessed a skill his father never had: patience. He'd learned from both his parents to strategize, not just jump in and let his heart lead. Dear Mom and Dad had allowed their emotions to rule. It had made Barrett's life a living hell until his father had passed five years ago and his mother had disappeared to South America with her fourth husband.

Slowly, he released a pent-up breath. He never imagined he would ever see Mina again. The owner of Róisín, Bridget Massey, had contacted him to ask if he would consider investing in her property. She'd had a solid proposal, numbers to back up her request. He'd wondered if Mina had moved back to Glenvarra, if he might encounter her on the streets, but had dismissed it. He wasn't going to turn down a deal simply because he might run into a former lover who may have stayed in London or moved somewhere else entirely.

But as soon as Bridget had started to tell him about Mina, her heritage consultant and event planner who had breathed new life into the hotel, he'd known. Known he had inadvertently tracked down the woman who still haunted his dreams and lingered at the edge of his conscience.

It had taken nearly an hour to make his decision. More time than he cared to admit he spent in deciding. Ultimately, he had decided the Róisín project was worth considering.

As for Mina, his trip to Glenvarra was supposed to prove that while his night with Mina had been enjoyable, it had only been one night. His continued thoughts of her were the result of unresolved anger and guilt.

Texting Mina and giving her a heads-up he would be in Glenvarra had been the right thing to do. But when she hadn't responded, he'd resisted following up with another text or a call. If she wanted to give him the silent treatment when he was extending an olive branch, then he wouldn't push. She would just have to deal with the surprise of seeing him at Róisín.

Except he had been the one shocked into silence.

A baby. His baby.

He turned toward the sea. Mina had spoken of Glenvarra more than once in London. Talked about the cliffs she would venture to when she needed to think, to take a few moments for herself. She'd said the ocean brought her peace.

But as he stared out over the dark water, he felt anything but peaceful. He wasn't used to making mistakes. Wasn't used to breaking his own rules, like letting down his guard or crossing a line with an employee.

And now there was a child.

Fury rose like the sharp-edged waves. He breathed in, let it fill him for one angry moment.

Then he released it. Reassumed control. Anger was volatile, wild. An emotion his parents had indulged in with regular frequency. They'd swung from the highest highs to the lowest lows in a matter of days, sometimes even hours.

In his earlier years, he'd sought out their time, their affection, trying to fill the pervasive hole in his heart. It had taken far longer than it should have for him to finally realize his parents would only pay attention to him when it suited their needs. He needed to rely on the only person he could count on: himself.

His parents' relationship had soured him on the ideas of getting married or having a family of his own. His dating life had reinforced that. Most women were content with the brief affairs he was willing to offer, laid out in explicit terms before the first date. But several had pushed for more, which led to tears, shouting matches, and on one memorable occasion, coming back to his penthouse to find his tailored suits cut to shreds.

So, he'd taken a break. A year-long break to focus on growing Sawyer Development, to enjoy the quiet of his own world where he and he alone was in control.

Until Sabrina Callahan had blazed into his office with a sunny smile that had drawn him in and a witty determination that commandeered his respect.

He'd told himself it had been too long since he'd dated. He'd been balancing numerous projects, had been spending longer and longer hours at the office. His defenses had been down.

Excuses. Poor ones that didn't change the fact that Mina was pregnant with his child.

His chest tightened. He knew nothing about kids, had never changed a diaper or given one a bottle. But he remembered with vivid clarity the empty seats at school events, the nights he'd waited for one or both of them to tuck him in until he'd finally pulled the blankets up to his chin and tried not to cry.

Mina had shared an unexpectedly vulnerable side that night in his office when she'd told him she never knew her father. She'd tried to brush it off, but he'd seen the pain in her eyes, heard the loss in her voice. He'd wanted to tear down the world to find the man and demand how he could leave his daughter like that.

They'd both known the pain of absent parents. He would never, ever let his child experience that. Just like he wouldn't let his child experience the chaos he'd lived with growing up. There had been wealth, plenty of toys and things and stuff. None of it had replaced having a parent who couldn't be bothered to show up for a recital or read him a story before bed.

He'd never imagined having a family of his own. He had zero interest in letting a woman in deep enough to even think about having a child together. Besides, how could he possibly be capable of being a father given the horrid example he'd grown up with? How could he let down his walls enough to give a child the kind of affection they deserved? The kind he'd once craved?

But now there was no choice. He would do the right thing.

He glanced to the left. Mina's vivid red-gold hair stood out against the gray landscape, much the way she had stood out in the austere offices of Sawyer Development. A flame he couldn't stay away from.

And then she disappeared around a large rock.

His gaze shifted to the turrets of Róisín by the Cliffs. He took control of the knots in his chest, refashioned them into hardened resolve. Mina was about to find out she was wrong. There was far more here in Glenvarra for him than she knew.

He could only imagine the blowup that would

ensue when she found out he was here to invest in the hotel.

He would secure the hotel deal. And then he and Mina were going to have a long conversation. One that would end with him being a part of their child's life whether Mina liked it or not.

CHAPTER THREE

Mina

THE WARMTH OF Róisín's grand hall wrapped around Mina like a blanket as the double doors closed behind her. Despite the icy raindrops clinging to her face, her cheeks were flushed, her skin hot. As soon as she'd rounded the rock on the trail, she'd quickened her pace, walking as quickly as she dared in case Barrett tried to catch up and continue their conversation.

Tears pricked her eyes. He'd looked good. So damn good standing there in his suit and peacoat, the wind tearing at his normally perfectly styled hair.

But it had been the shock in his eyes, the unexpected hurt, that had cut. Of all the reactions she'd anticipated, Barrett wanting to be involved hadn't even been a consideration. Anger, denial, or offering money while she raised the child on her own had seemed more likely.

When he'd said he wanted to be involved, that he wasn't going to back down, hope had kindled in her chest. The tiniest flare, but it had burned for a brief, bright moment.

Until he'd snuffed it out in typical Barrett Sawyer fashion.

I always fulfill my obligations.

Anger surged. "My child is not an obligation," she muttered under her breath as she untied her cloak.

The baby dug a heel into her belly, as if protesting the rapid beating of her heart.

"It's all right." Mina settled a hand over her stomach and rubbed slow, soothing circles. "It's going to be all right."

She said it not just for the baby but herself, too. Barrett would be back. He wouldn't give up so easily. She just needed to get herself back under control, achieve that sense of cold neutrality she'd managed to portray on the trail before she dealt with him again.

Heat pricked her eyes. Again. If he wanted to be involved, truly involved, she couldn't deny him that. Her child could have a father. Something she herself had craved for so many years. No matter how much she wanted Barrett Sawyer out of her life, letting him in was the right thing to do.

But if he insisted on treating her baby like a business deal instead of a person, she would cut him out before he could even blink. No father was better than a father who was cold or indifferent.

She would never let her child experience the kind of pain she'd felt that morning in his office.

Stay strong, stay firm.

Barrett Sawyer was not known for negotiating. But if he was truly going to try his hand at being a parent, she would be the one to set the terms of their arrangement. It was time he learned he couldn't always have his way.

With that resolution in mind, she walked farther into the hall.

Scarlet carpet edged in gold covered most of the floor. Dark strips of limestone had been left visible near the walls, a recommendation Mina had made when Bridget had hired her to feature the original flooring of the castle. Pale cream walls emphasized the dramatic dark wood ceiling, punctuated by Waterford crystal chandeliers. Thick gold chairs were trimmed in the same rich brown oak as the ceiling and covered with burgundy-colored vines that twisted and twined across the fabric.

A history lover's dream. Every detail honored the legacy of the castle and the town that had supported it for over four hundred years.

Mina trailed a hand across one of the stone pillars holding up the arch leading into the reception area. The roughness of the stone, the grooves carved hundreds of years ago by a mason's chisel, soothed her.

She loved Glenvarra, from the winding cobblestone streets to the harbor dotted with tour boats that ferried vacationers up and down the coastline during the warmer months. She loved the balance of luxury and quiet refinement, the mix of restaurants and shops against the backdrop of Irish farmland.

Mama and her grandmother had brought her to Róisín for tea, lunch, and a horseback ride for her twelfth birthday. Her lips curved into a small smile. The castle had been her first love. She'd read every book, spent hours in the library poring over letters and diaries of past occupants. And now her current role allowed her to connect not only with the history of the castle and surrounding countryside but the guests, too.

Unlike the rapid pace of life in London, her world here combined luxury with contentment, allowed her to build relationships and dig far deeper than her fleeting assignments for Sawyer Development had permitted.

Her heart twisted despite her resolve. Had she done the right thing not telling Barrett? There were letters, a dozen or so, in the drawer of her desk at home. She had written the first the day she found out she was pregnant, the second after her first ultrasound. And every time she thought about mailing them, she remembered the cold fury in his eyes, the disgusted twist of his lips. So, the letters had sat, growing with every milestone.

"Hey, Mina."

Mina turned and smiled as Thomas Mallory stopped next to her. Only a couple inches taller than her, with fluffy blond hair and thick, muscled arms, he reminded her of a bright-eyed teddy bear.

When she'd come back from Austria last week, she'd sought out Thomas, one of her closest friends since primary school. She'd told him about the inheritance and the marriage clause. It had seemed like the perfect solution to ask Thomas to marry her for a year. A platonic marriage, one that would end with her giving him three million euros.

Thomas had asked for time to think about her proposal. His reticence had surprised her, but she'd respected his request. Still, it was hard not to push for an answer.

"Hey."

Thomas's brown eyes narrowed. "What's wrong?"

"Why does anything have to be wrong?"

"I know you, Sabrina Boann Callahan. Don't lie to me."

Why, Mina wondered for the dozenth time, couldn't she have been attracted to a man like Thomas? Someone kind and gentle. But there had never been desire or attraction with Thomas. He was like family.

Barrett Sawyer, on the other hand, had introduced her to a passion she'd never experienced before. But he was definitely not the kind of man she should fall in love with either. Besides, he didn't believe in love or marriage or family. Sentiments he'd expressed several times and reinforced by dating a series of stunning but self-absorbed women. Every time he went to a gala or a ribbon cutting or whatever event ridiculously wealthy people attended, there was always someone new on his arm. A trend Mina was certain he had continued after she left London, although she hadn't had the guts to look him up online.

She released a long, slow breath. "Barrett's here. He showed up on my walk."

Thomas slowly looked down at her stomach, then back at her. "So I guess he knows now."

"He does."

"And?"

"He wants to be involved." She shot Thomas a glare as a smug smile crossed his face. "Don't you dare say I told you so."

Thomas was the only one she had confided Barrett's identity to when she'd found out she was pregnant. He had also pushed for her to contact Barrett and tell him about the baby. It was the first and only time she could remember them arguing.

"I'm not saying a thing." His smile disappeared. "So what does this mean for your…proposal?"

"Not a thing." When Thomas continued to stare at her, she put one hand on her hip. "What?"

"So, you're going to enter into a coparenting relationship with the father of your child while marrying your best friend for a multimillion-pound inheritance?"

Mina groaned. "It sounds like one of those romance movies that come out around the holidays."

Before Thomas could reply, the radio clipped to his belt crackled.

"Thomas? The lights in the Grand Ballroom are flickering. Could you come check?"

Mina grimaced. The Autumn Heritage Banquet, the largest event she had planned to date, was to be hosted in the Grand Ballroom next weekend. The last thing she needed was electric problems ahead of the gala that hosted some of the most well-known public figures in the United Kingdom.

Thomas slid a thick arm around Mina's shoulders and gave her a quick squeeze. "We'll talk later, okay?"

"Okay."

She watched him walk off, her brow furrowed. When she'd come back from the will reading in Austria last week, Thomas had been the first person she'd sought out. She'd told him everything, from the will and the marriage clause to her two new cousins, and finished with her proposal. One year of marriage in name only. They'd travel to Dublin so no one in Glenvarra would know but them. When they crossed the year mark, they'd obtain a divorce, and he'd walk away with three million euros.

But Thomas had surprised her by asking for

time to think about it. There was something he wasn't telling her. She was trying to be patient, but his hesitance stung.

"Mina!"

Mina turned and smiled as a petite woman with a strawberry-blond bob walked toward her with bouncing steps. Bridget Massey, the owner of Róisín, had just celebrated her fiftieth birthday, but she could easily pass for a woman in her late thirties with her heart-shaped face, sparkling eyes and an energy that never seemed to quit.

"Hi, Bridget."

"How are the cliffs?"

"Beautiful. Wild."

"It truly is a magical place, is it not?" Bridget's smile dimmed as her voice trailed off.

Mina frowned. "Is everything all right?"

Bridget shook her head. "Just feeling nostalgic. Hard to believe it's been twenty years since I took over."

Mina glanced around at the freshly painted walls, the new furniture, and the historic oil paintings. "And look what you've accomplished."

"Yes." Bridget nodded firmly. "And we have plenty more coming." She glanced down at her watch, then looked around the room before edging closer to Mina. "Speaking of, I have a meeting today with someone about financing the renovation of the North Wing."

Warning bells clanged in Mina's head. Surely it couldn't be. "Oh?" she managed.

"I haven't told anyone yet. I don't want to get my own hopes up," Bridget added with a laugh. "Especially not anyone else's. You're the only one I've told."

Dread tasted bitter on Mina's tongue. "Who is it?"

Bridget started to answer, then glanced over Mina's shoulder. "Mr. Sawyer!"

Mina's stomach dropped just as the baby did a roll. The combination threw her off balance, forcing her to mentally root herself to the floor before she slowly turned to face the bane of her existence.

Barrett strode across the lobby, attracting more than one appreciative female glance as he moved, his peacoat draped over one arm and his shoulders thrown back, showing off the perfection of his hand-tailored suit. Slate gray with a black tie, as if he had brought the storm with him when he arrived in Glenvarra.

As he walked toward Bridget, he glanced around with his usual cool confidence, as if he already envisioned himself owning the place.

Mina cast a quick look at Bridget, but Bridget was walking toward Barrett with a big smile on her face and didn't notice Mina's reaction.

What was Bridget thinking? Surely she knew how Barrett operated. Yes, he offered thousands up to millions in financing, but it always came with a price. He would demand a share of her business. Once he staked his claim, he would never let go.

Bridget shook Barrett's hand warmly. Barrett smiled down at her.

Alarms scattered up Mina's spine. Surely Bridget was not signing a contract today.

But what if she was?

Mina walked forward, forcing herself to take slow, measured steps.

Bridget turned and smiled at her. "Mina, I would like to introduce you to someone."

Mina forced a smile to her face as Barrett turned his attention to her, challenge glinting in his eyes. She made a quick, calculated decision. Better to step forward and deliver the first surprise than allow Barrett to take control of the narrative.

"Of course. Mr. Sawyer and I have already met." She inclined her head. "Welcome to Róisín by the Cliffs, Mr. Sawyer."

CHAPTER FOUR

Barrett

BARRETT BARELY CONTAINED his surprise at Mina's pronouncement. He had expected her to run or at least pretend not to know him. Reluctant admiration for her boldness took root inside him. But really, based on his experience with her back in London, was it any surprise that she would rise to the challenge?

He took her hand. Awareness shot up his arm, followed by a streak of possessiveness that tightened his muscles. It was the first time he had touched her in seven months.

The answering shock in her eyes pleased him. At least he wasn't the only one going through this hell. And if she was still having a reaction to him, that meant he had an in. He just needed more time to talk to her, to convince her that letting him be involved was the right thing for everyone.

His hand tightened around hers, a promise that he was not going anywhere.

Mina's jaw hardened, her only sign of defiance.

It wouldn't be easy persuading her to let him in. But even though it would be easier if she just agreed, he couldn't deny the spark of excitement at the challenge that lay before him. He had gotten used to people bowing, agreeing to his every whim.

But not Sabrina Callahan. She hadn't cared if her opinion aligned with his or not. He'd started to look forward to their meetings, to verbally sparring with her and watching the color rise in her cheeks as she matched her wits against his.

Too much, he reminded himself. He'd enjoyed himself far too much. He'd let her in bit by bit without even realizing it. And then, when he should have done the right thing and turned away, he'd crossed the one line he swore he'd always stand firm against and slept with an employee.

He released her hand and stepped back. All those years doing what he could to not follow in his father's footsteps, and it only took one feisty intern to bring him down. A fact he needed to keep in mind. He'd given in to a moment of weakness, a mistake he would not make again.

"I'm sorry," Bridget said, glancing between the two of them. "I didn't realize you knew each other."

"I worked for Sawyer Development for a few months while I was in London," Mina replied, "as an intern."

Bridget's brows drew together. "I don't recall seeing that on your curriculum vitae."

A blush stole over Mina's cheeks. "I'm sorry. I—" She slanted a cool glance at Barrett. "Mr. Sawyer runs a very respectable firm, but we disagreed on several issues. I wasn't sure what kind of recommendation I would get should anyone decide to check, so I decided to leave it off."

Another thing he had always respected, even if he had not always liked it: her blunt honesty. Although he suspected her honesty to be twofold. Not only was she being honest, she was taking control of the story.

Two could play at that game.

"We may have disagreed," he added, "but Miss Callahan did excellent work in her time with us."

The line of worry between Bridget's brows disappeared. "So, it won't be a problem for you to work together?"

Barrett looked at Mina. "Not at all."

He could practically see the steam coming out of her ears. "No," Mina added.

It was a wonder Bridget did not hear the underlying tension in her voice or note the muscles standing out in her neck.

"Good." Bridget gestured toward a dark oak door with a gold plaque. "In that case, Mina, if you have ten minutes, would you mind joining us? Mr. Sawyer is here to talk about some exciting updates for the castle."

Mina

Mina forced herself to smile even though it felt more like stretching her lips across her teeth into a horrid grimace that wasn't fooling anyone. Fortunately, Bridget did not seem to notice.

But judging by the amused quirk of his lips, Barrett knew. He gestured for her to go before him.

Showing her emotions would not get her anywhere with Barrett. He considered feelings to be a weakness. He had taught her a valuable lesson when it came to business and her personal life: less transparency, fewer emotions. So, she would just have to stuff the turmoil swirling around inside her as deep as she could and be a professional.

She inclined her head. "Thank you, Mr. Sawyer."

She quietly savored the surprise in his eyes as she walked by with her head held high.

When she was inside Bridget's office, she started to shrug off her cloak.

"If I may, Miss Callahan."

She could not object without appearing rude. Mina nodded, then barely stopped a gasp from escaping as Barrett's fingertips brushed down her upper arms while he pulled the cloak away.

Before she could stop it, her mind flashed back to that night. The moment she had seen the pale light spilling out of his office, had stopped in the doorway and looked in to see him on the couch, one hand braced against his forehead and the other clutching a pen as he stared down at some document. He looked tired but approachable, and as always, ridiculously handsome. She had hesitated on the threshold.

And then she had crossed it.

Things would have been so different if she had simply kept walking.

She swallowed hard. "Thank you."

Despising the huskiness in her voice, she took a seat in one of the plush chairs in front of Bridget's desk. Out of the corner of her eye, she caught Barrett glancing at her rounded belly as he sat next to her.

You have nothing to feel guilty about. You have nothing to feel guilty about.

Maybe if she repeated it enough times, she would start to believe it herself.

"Congratulations, by the way."

Her eyes widened as her head snapped around. "What?"

A slow, arrogant smile spread across his face. "The baby."

Oh, he really is doing this. The snake.

He settled into the chair and crossed one ankle over his knee, the epitome of a wealthy professional making casual conversation. "Boy or girl?"

"I want it to be a surprise," she said faintly.

"When are you due?"

"Around New Year's." She turned to Bridget, cutting him off. "So, what is this new venture?"

Bridget folded her hands, excited energy practically vibrating off her small frame. "You know how long I've wanted to renovate the North Wing." She sighed. "I finally got the estimate. I can't afford it. It's nearly nine million euros."

Shocked, Mina glanced at the painting hanging on the wall of Róisín by the Cliffs before the fire had gutted much of the North Wing in the early nineteen hundreds. Even when she had been a child coming up to Róisín for tea, she remembered Bridget sharing her dream of one day restoring the castle to its full glory.

But nine million?

Mina turned back around to face Barrett, who was watching her very carefully. A chill whispered across the back of her neck. It always unsettled her how he looked at her, like he could see past her smiles and sunny optimism to the darker parts of her soul. Like he could see the loneliness of the missing half of her history, a hole she had tried to fill over the years with her research and work. When they talked, disagreed, even argued, he still listened to her every word with an attentiveness that had felt like an intimate caress.

She hadn't had much experience with dating. She'd gone on a few dates in secondary school. There'd been a nice boy she'd dated for several months in college, but he'd finally grown tired of her prioritizing her studies over going out and having fun.

One day, she'd promised herself, she'd make time to date. Find the right man, fall in love, get married. Start to heal the wounds of her past by creating the family she'd dreamed of for years.

Except there'd always been something else to accomplish, something else to do. She'd made the thirty-minute drive to Dublin four days a week for four years as she worked toward her undergraduate degree, and then for two more years as she pursued an advanced degree. She'd worked weekends in the restaurant at Róisín and spent her graduate years interning with the Heritage Council of Ireland.

And no matter how hard she studied, no matter how many hours she devoted to her work, the emptiness persisted. An emptiness that, for one night, she had forgotten about as she had revealed some of her deepest secrets with a man she had never thought capable of understanding. A man she had felt compelled to confide in, who had once again given her his attention, his dark eyes never straying from her face. He hadn't told her it would all sort itself out, like Thomas, or asked if they could talk about this another time, like her mother. Once again, he'd listened. And she had fallen just a little bit in love with Barrett Sawyer.

Crazy. She had been absolutely crazy. They had both been lonely, consenting adults who had let hormones take the lead. She would be a fool to believe that a man like Barrett, a man who preferred short-term relationships and avoided commitments like marriage, had actually cared.

Focus.

"So, you've offered to invest." At Barrett's nod, Mina arched a brow. "Isn't Glenvarra outside your usual area, Mr. Sawyer?"

"I contacted him." Bridget glanced at the painting, too. "I read a profile on Mr. Sawyer in a magazine and the work he does."

"We've done some work in Dublin and Galway, but I've been wanting to expand Sawyer Development's reach," Barrett injected smoothly, "so this opportunity benefits us both."

And your bank account.

Even if Bridget had invited Barrett to Glenvarra, it still didn't explain why he had texted Mina last week.

"I invited Mr. Sawyer to Róisín so he could see the hotel firsthand, examine the accounts, and get a better idea of what makes us unique. He'll be staying the week and joining us for the Autumn Heritage Banquet." Bridget beamed as she looked at Barrett. "It's an event Mina came up with to serve not only our guests here at the castle but at other hotels and bed-and-breakfasts in the area. A night of historic Irish food, music performances, a live auction featuring work by local artisans, and dancing. A portion of the proceeds is going to an artists consortium here in Glenvarra. I think you're really going to enjoy it."

"I'm sure I will."

Mina's fingers curled into the fabric of her dress. "How nice you'll be joining us, Mr. Sawyer."

Bridget must have heard the strain in Mina's voice because she gave Mina an odd look but thankfully said nothing.

"I'm looking forward to it," Barrett said. "Bridget has spoken highly of your work."

So that was how he knew Mina was here. Was this it? All just some horrible coincidence? Bridget had reached out to Barrett to request financing, mentioned Mina's name, and Barrett had connected the dots?

"I greatly enjoy my work here."

And she did. It was the perfect blend of her love of history and research while sharing it with others and making it fun. Who knew that her dream career had been here in Glenvarra the whole time?

"Speaking of that," Bridget said as she leaned forward, "I have another favor to ask. Would you have availability this week to escort Mr. Sawyer around and show him what you do? Maybe take him on a tour or on one of the castle's exclusive experiences? Normally I wouldn't ask ahead of an event, but since you mentioned all the details had been confirmed and the staff were taking care of so much, I was hoping you'd be free."

It was like being trapped in a prison cell with the walls lowly closing in. But a quick glance confirmed that the sunny yellow walls of Bridget's office were still in the same place and that bars had not, in fact, formed over the windows.

One look at Bridget's face and Mina knew she couldn't say no. Not only was this her job, but she couldn't snuff out that hope. She owed Bridget so much, and she wanted the renovation, not just for Bridget, but for Róisín and the town. Where else was Bridget going to get that kind of money? Who else would take that kind of risk?

Inspiration hit.

Just two weeks ago, Mina would have had to simply sit back and watch as Barrett slithered his way in. But she had a multimillion euro inheritance within reach. Just enough that she could cover the repairs at Róisín. She needed to talk to Thomas, explain why his yes mattered even more now. Once they married, her inheritance would be guaranteed. And after converting the money from euros to pounds, even with the promised payout to Thomas, the remaining amount would still be enough to cover the renovation and leave a couple million for her, the baby and her mom.

She could offer it as a loan or find some other way of turning it into a business offer. Calculating how much she would have left, she would even be willing to offer it as a gift, although she imagined Bridget's pride and sense of responsibility would not allow her to accept it as such. Those details could be worked out later.

For this week, she would play nice with Barrett, use the time to clear the air with him, and show him how Róisín and Glenvarra were not the kind of places that matched Sawyer Development's usual investments. She would find a time in the next day or two to float her idea to Bridget.

By the end of the week, Róisín's future would be secure.

"No, Bridget." Mina turned and smiled at Barrett. "I don't mind at all."

CHAPTER FIVE

Barrett

MINA WAS UP to something. Her smile was too sweet, the gleam in her eye too bright.

Barrett inclined his head even as alarm bells clanged. "Thank you, Miss Callahan."

Mina was far too determined to simply give in. It was one of the traits he had liked about her ever since he met her. She never cowed to him, much as she might think he wanted her to. Even though he had disagreed with some of her recommendations, it had been obvious that she cared about her work. He'd been impressed by her gumption and passion.

Yet he'd also seen the shock on the faces of some of his long-term employees the first time she disagreed with him in a meeting. It was as if the entire room had waited with bated breath to see how he would respond.

He tapped his fingers against his leg. It had been the first indication his staff saw him as unapproachable—a notion that had crawled under his skin and sat there, sharp and grating, ever since. No, he didn't have his father's jovial demeanor. But he'd always tried to engage with his employees, asked for honesty. Yet not one of them had ever talked to him the way Mina had.

He'd tried to make changes over the last few months, tried to engage more, even smile now and again. But the stark contrast between how Mina had treated him compared to everyone else persisted.

It hadn't helped, he thought grimly, that as his respect for Mina had grown, so too had his attraction. An attraction he wasn't even aware of until she'd stood in his doorway that night, dim lighting creating shadows across her face and a kind, concerned smile just for him.

He swallowed a sudden burst of anger. Anger at her, yes, but anger at himself, too. She hadn't stopped to seduce him. He knew that, even though he'd made the grave mistake of insinuating just that the morning after the board meeting. No, Mina had stopped to check on him because, at her core, Mina was a kind person.

He'd felt the spark from across the room, hadn't even tried to stop the warmth that spread when she'd come in to look at the proposal he was working on. There had been so many opportunities to send her away that night. Instead, selfish bastard he was, he'd soaked up every moment.

And then there'd been the kiss.

She'd drifted over to the window sometime around midnight as rain pattered against the glass. Silhouetted against the London cityscape drenched in rain and night, she brought every suppressed longing in him to the surface. He'd joined her, standing by her side, acutely aware of her perfume, her soft exhale. He'd glanced down at her just as she looked up at him. Her lips had parted. He'd leaned down. Inhaled sharply when he'd felt the warmth of her body just before he slanted his mouth over hers.

He'd been the one to initiate their affair. Ultimately it was his responsibility, not hers. But she should've still told him about the baby.

His anger grew. Would she have truly gone through with it? Had the baby, raised it without him ever knowing? Especially after what she'd gone through as a child?

She had confided in him so much that night. As they ate noodles and crab rangoon with chopsticks, Mina had told him that she never knew who her father was. Didn't know what he'd done for a living, how he and her mother had met. Mina had shared that as she focused on her box of steamed rice. But he'd still heard the pain, seen the sadness on her face when she'd finally looked at him.

And yet Mina had been prepared to do the exact same thing to their son or daughter?

"If you have time, a tour this afternoon would

be a good way to start," he said. "Get the feel of the castle."

Mina's nostrils flared. "I do have some time, although I'm hosting a tea in the library at two."

He glanced at the clock on the wall. "I have some business to discuss with Bridget, but it shouldn't take long. I'll come find you after and see if you're free."

There was nothing she could say that wouldn't invite questions or attention. So, Mina simply nodded, even though he was certain she was envisioning ways to torture him.

She stood. His eyes dropped down to her belly. A different heat stole over him—not anger, but protectiveness.

Had there been any complications? Had she been sick in the beginning? He was furious with her. But he hated that she'd been doing this alone for nearly seven months.

His mind flashed back to how he'd first seen her on the cliff, gazing out over the ocean as if she had only herself to depend on in this world. He'd recognized it. It was how he felt most of the time. Most days it didn't bother him. It had been routine ever since he'd been a child.

But there were days, and especially nights, where the emptiness stretched, yawning and deep, reminding him that he had no one else in this world. And he hated the thought of Mina experiencing that same sense of loneliness.

As she walked out, he resolved in that moment that no matter their past disagreements, he would show her that he wasn't like her father. He wasn't going to desert her or the baby.

The door closed with a click. Doubt flickered, but he stamped it out. He'd never lost before. He certainly wasn't going to now.

Mina

Books covered the walls, lovingly cradled by gleaming oak shelves that soared twenty feet toward the ceiling. Ivory drapes were open to the storm. In the warmer months, the drapes would be burgundy or midnight blue, but Bridget switched them out in the winter to create a sensation of light as the darkness crept in earlier.

Normally the warm, glowing lamps and crackling fireplace would have soothed Mina. But as she turned and stomped down the length of the library for the dozenth time, she was anything but calm. Barrett had been with Bridget for over an hour. Afternoon tea was about to commence. Even now kitchen staff were straightening tablecloths and setting delicate teacups on china plates in the center of the library.

Mina had come up with the event a couple months ago, a way to combine history with an indoor activity that would provide guests with something else to do during the colder months. Various teas were served along with traditional

Irish foods. Mina would begin with a few facts about tea and Ireland, including how it had been a luxury item out of reach for so many. She loved sharing the stories, imagining the trade routes between Ireland and Britain.

But now, instead of reviewing her facts, all she could think about was what Barrett was accomplishing in his quest to invest in Róisín. She should have said something before she left. What if Bridget had already signed the contract?

The baby gave her a sharp kick.

"Shh, child." Mina placed a hand on her belly and started to rub slow, soothing circles. No matter what happened, she would persevere. She may not have as much money as Barrett did, but at least she had some, enough to cover the renovation costs for Róisín. She could, and would, fight.

Her hair prickled on the back of her neck. She turned to see Barrett in the doorway watching her. She swallowed hard against the intensity of his gaze. "How was your meeting, Mr. Sawyer?"

"Successful."

She cleared her throat. "Did she sign?"

"No."

Mina barely stopped herself from sagging in relief. "Well..." She smiled. "I'm about to host the afternoon tea. I'll be available in an hour for the tour."

His eyes gleamed like a predator. "I just purchased a ticket at the front desk."

If it weren't for the presence of the staff in the room, Mina would have told him exactly where he could spend the next hour, and it certainly wasn't anywhere near her.

The waiters straightened the last table before they headed out, leaving her and Barrett alone in the library.

"Be sure to try the Assam. It's one of my favorites. Considered to be very strong."

He stared at her for a moment. "Noted."

"We'll start at two on the dot." She started to turn away.

Warm fingers wrapped around her wrist. She froze, slowly turning back to look at him. The emotion in his eyes shocked her. Determination, yes, but also a sorrow she hadn't expected to see. A small crack worked its way through her resolve.

"You're not doing this alone."

"Threats may have made you successful in London, but they won't get you anywhere here."

With a quick tug, Barrett pulled her to him. He leaned down, his mouth mere inches from hers. "It's not a threat, Sabrina. It's a promise."

It had been months since they had been this close; six months and three weeks, to be exact. She noticed now, just as she had then, the dark stubble on his jaw, the hollows beneath his cheekbones. His eyes dropped down to her lips. Her breath hitched.

But before she could even begin to analyze what

she was thinking or feeling, Barrett released her and stepped back.

God, what a fool she was. For one moment she'd imagined tenderness, remembered what they had had together. Regardless of the softer side she'd glimpsed in his office, in spite of the sweetness he had shown that night, it had been just that—one night.

Her mother had made the same mistake, falling for a man she'd met while vacationing in France one summer and hoping he would eventually settle down. That had been the one detail Mama had confided.

But her mother had also been strong. She hadn't pined for Jakob, hadn't wasted away for him. She'd come back to Glenvarra and given birth to her daughter with only her mother by her side. She'd worked two jobs while going to nursing school. No, she hadn't made it to all of Mina's school events. But she'd shown up when she could and had never let Mina forget that she was loved and wanted.

And now Mina needed to have that same strength.

She straightened her shoulders. "Mr. Sawyer, you can take your ticket and—"

"Careful, Sabrina," Barrett interrupted. "You have guests."

Mina froze as the sound of muted voices

reached her ears. A moment later people started to filter into the library.

Furious with him, and herself for losing control, she turned away from him and walked toward her guests with a smile pasted firmly on her face.

For the next hour, she was Mina Callahan, heritage consultant and events planner for Róisín Castle. It was the role she had secured for herself, part of the identity she had crafted in the aftermath of heartbreak.

She liked the life she had created, and she was excited for the life to come. She wouldn't let anyone, including her former lover, ruin that.

CHAPTER SIX

Barrett

The hotel was impressive. So far Mina had taken him through the the restaurant, the bar, a signature tower suite, and a standard suite. Every room had been clean and decorated with a combination of historical paintings and furniture while still offering modern convenience.

When Bridget had first reached out to him, he'd had concerns about the amount she requested, even though she'd provided ample records demonstrating the hotel's ability to turn a profit—quite a lot for a hotel in a small coastal village. But it was obvious that Bridget's hard work and the staff she'd hired to implement her vision were paying off.

The tower suite they were currently standing in took up two levels of one of the castle's turrets, offering stunning views of the ocean and coastline. Some of the arrow-slit windows had been retained, along with the limestone walls. The oak-beam ceilings gleamed, and the hand-carved four-poster bed was something he could easily picture a lord of the castle sleeping in hundreds of years ago.

His lips quirked. He wasn't usually given to daydreaming. Perhaps it was the castle. Or, he thought with a glance at Mina, perhaps it was her. Her design skills had been another talent he'd appreciated about her. Whether it was a historical renovation or one of his preferred new builds, Mina had always been able to visualize, to bring a space to life.

Given that she had an undergraduate degree in architecture and a master's degree in building conservation, he knew her studies had trended more toward practical conservation. But she had an eye for design, for color, and of course, history. Mina had done good work for Sawyer Development, and as much as their parting had been acrimonious, he respected Bridget for snapping Mina up when she had the chance.

Another point in Bridget's favor: she not only hired talent, she retained them. It made the possibility of investing in her business seem even more attractive.

The sky darkened as another storm moved toward the coast.

His father had been the opposite, specializing in finding sad cases, be they businesses or properties. He built them up, took all the profits he could, and then abandoned them, leaving them to flounder with repair costs, taxes, or any of the other fees that could come up out of nowhere and smother a business.

He glanced over his shoulder at Mina, who was still pointing out details like the freestanding marble soaking tub and ambient lighting designed to look like candlelight. She'd pulled her hair up into a loose bun, leaving her face bare to his gaze.

He knew she didn't like how he always had a stake in whatever companies he invested in. The first time he'd told her, she'd wrinkled her nose at him. He'd been both irritated and amused.

What he hadn't told her was that having a stake in the companies he invested in wasn't just about control. He would never make his father's selfish mistakes. When he invested in a company, it wasn't just to turn a profit. He wanted to build those businesses up, see them succeed the way Sawyer Development had. On more than one occasion, his stake in a business had enabled him to step in and provide additional support long after the initial work was done. It didn't always work, but it was better than the alternative.

Mina pushed a button on the wall, and a recessed door opened, revealing an in-room safe. "Modern amenities," she rattled off, "including the safe, high-speed fiber connectivity, and in-room media access. All carefully hidden to maintain the historic feel of the room while still offering our guests convenience and luxury."

"Do you find that people really care about the historic elements?"

His question worked; Mina's head snapped to the side, her eyes flashing with blue fire. He shouldn't needle her. But he couldn't help enjoying the visual battle playing across her face, from the tightening of her lips to the deep inhale through her nose. Finally, she gave a slight nod.

"Not everyone." She gestured to a plaque on the wall near the entryway. "We installed the historic preservation plaques in every room toward the end of summer. They detail what in the room is original to the castle, any historic replicas, things of that nature. Multiple guests have shared it's enhanced their stay and made them appreciate what's in the room."

"Was that your idea?"

"It was."

She was good. Very, very good.

He missed this, he realized with a jolt. Missed her ideas, her insight. The summer intern who'd come in after her wasn't half as good.

Correction, he amended to himself. They were good, but they lacked Mina's passion.

Mina blinked and looked away as a delicate blush stole over her cheeks.

Satisfaction had him pressing his lips together so she wouldn't see his smile. No, she was most definitely not immune to him.

A stray curl slipped out of her bun and drifted

down to lie against her neck. His hand came up of its own accord just before he caught himself and forced his arm back down. The most concerning thing about his interest in Mina was that it went beyond simple physical desire.

Yes, there had been that initial admiration of a beautiful face, that quiet spark of attraction. But Mina was the first woman he had wanted to get to know on a deeper level. The first woman he'd wanted to touch just because he wanted to.

Even now, after all these months, she was still dangerous.

He turned back to the window and glanced to the right toward the North Wing. Unlike the tower they were standing in, the North Wing's towers were a jumbled mess of fallen, scorched stone.

"Are we allowed to look at the North Wing?"

"Why?"

He looked back over at her, arms crossed and her chin held high. Stubborn, frustrated, yet soldiering on. One key difference between her and his mother. His mother had been all too happy to let others deal with her problems. On the few occasions she'd been confronted with her behavior, she'd descended into tears, hysterics, or both.

"I like to see what I'm investing in."

She blinked but didn't say anything more as she led him out.

A few minutes later they stood outside the ruins of the North Wing. Normally the sight of old buildings falling into ruin didn't bother him. Progress necessitated change. Too often people, like his parents, clung to the past instead of moving forward. Whether it was their wasteful spending on Regency and Georgian-era artifacts or bringing up each other's numerous affairs, they had thrived on the memories of what had been instead of living in the present.

But as Barrett looked up at the broken windows and twisted metal latticework, at the ivy creeping up the walls and the wild grass pushing through the cracks, there was a sense of loss, a feeling that something valuable had been taken.

He shrugged it off as Mina began her recitation.

"The wing originally functioned as garrison quarters. There was a watchtower room at the top, rooms for fish, kelp ash, and wine casks." She slid on the same cloak she'd been wearing when he first spied her on the cliffs as she looked up at the ruined roof. "The top of the tower could be seen for miles."

He glanced down at the floor, then frowned as he caught sight of a large, jagged crack running from one corner of the floor up part of a wall. "Has this been looked into?"

"I'm sure it has." He looked over his shoulder in time to see Mina's glower. "Bridget has the North Wing evaluated every year by an engineering team out of Dublin for structural integrity."

He straightened, making a mental note to review Bridget's last engineering report. He'd done enough construction work in his early years with Sawyer Development as he worked his way up to recognize that something was off.

But he'd have that conversation with Bridget. Mina would most likely assume he was just coming up with excuses to demolish instead of renovate.

"Bridget said she wants to turn the North Wing into more affordable guest quarters," he mentioned.

"That's right."

"What do you think?"

Warring emotions flashed across Mina's face. Slowly she looked away from him and back to the wing. Her face softened as her eyes slid over the ruins.

His heart twisted. He'd initially found her sentimentality for old buildings naive. He'd accepted the need for a heritage consultant, even if it had created more obstacles and headaches along the way. But he had come to miss her dedication and emotion.

"I love what Róisín currently offers. But I also love the idea of us being able to offer this experience to those who may not be able to afford luxury. The couple that just got married. A family wanting to give their kids a memorable vacation." She looked back at him, challenge flaring in her eyes. "Why should that experience only be available to the wealthy?"

He inclined his head. "A fair point. But will it hold up economically?"

"Bridget's very good with numbers. I trust her completely."

The implication hung in the air between them. She trusted Bridget, but not him.

"How did the fire happen?"

"It's a bit of a legend, actually. Dating back to World War I." Mina looked out to the sea. "The Fitzpatrick family lived in this castle when World War I broke out. They had three sons, all of whom went to fight on the front." She paused, sucked in a breath. "All three were killed in France."

For a moment there was nothing but the distant roar of the ocean and the sensation of cold, damp raindrops clinging to the grass before slowly soaking into his shoes.

"The oldest son had been engaged to marry his childhood sweetheart." Mina craned her head back and looked up to the sky. "She would frequently climb up to the tower. Some said it was simply to be by herself while she waited for news. Others said it was to watch for her fiancé. But one night, she swore that his ghost visited her, told her that he had been killed in battle. Heartbroken, she destroyed the tower. Ripped curtains down, turned furniture over. In the process, she knocked over a candle that caught one of the drapes on fire."

"Is it true?"

"The fire did start in the tower of the North Wing." Mina glanced back at the hotel. "There was a partially burned letter between the eldest Fitzpatrick son and his fiancée. I've read it several times." Her voice softened to a near whisper. "They were truly in love. It's not hard to imagine the legend is true."

He glanced up at the darkening sky. His parents had insisted they loved each other like that: completely, irrevocably. That deep dedication to each other had caused far more problems than any good it created.

"What would you do?" he asked.

Mina frowned. "What would I do?" she repeated.

"Yes."

Mina almost looked guilty. "Bridget's plan is the one that matters."

He stepped closer, noting the quickening of her breath, the rise and fall of her chest beneath the material of her cloak. Her lips parted as her eyes dropped down to his mouth, then darted back up again.

"Bridget obviously trusts you. Values your opinion." He eased closer, stopping within a foot of her. "So, what would you do?"

Mina's teeth sank into her lower lip. "If money wasn't a concern? Renovation." She sighed. "That's the dream. But I looked at the engineering report. A partial renovation with a rebuild would be the best option, if not an entire rebuild."

Barrett paused, waiting a moment before speaking again. "Why rebuild here but not the town house?"

Mina stiffened. "You read the report I submitted before that staff meeting when you announced you would be demolishing the town house. It was a shorter version of the report I submitted to the risk and compliance officer. You knew my concerns and, when I tried to bring them up in the meeting, basically told me to be quiet. Not once before had you ever treated me like that. You ignored every recommendation I made."

"I'm the CEO. I'm allowed to make decisions as I see fit."

"I'm sorry," Mina snapped. "I must have missed the part in my job description where I was supposed to look the other way when you decide my work doesn't align with your goals."

"That property was not statutorily listed. There were no historical designations."

"But it wasn't just a building. It was a cultural artifact. It had unaltered window bays, original wrought-iron balconies, and—"

"I know all about the property," Barrett bit out.

It had been his father's first acquisition, acquired on the whim of his father's current mistress. He'd had no plans for it. He'd simply bought it—with money siphoned from one of Sawyer Development's accounts—because the woman had wanted it. But his father had failed to take any of the necessary steps in actually preserving the building. Instead, he sank money into the property, bordering on a million by the time all was said and done. Not on important things like structural supports but on new floors, drapes, art. One of the contractors his dad had hired had been injured working on the unpermitted projects. By some miracle, none of it had come to light. If it had, Sawyer Development would have been done for.

Now, Barrett just wanted the damned building gone. The last remaining link to his tumultuous past.

"I acknowledge the historic significance of the property. But it was still cheaper to demolish and rebuild, and I had approval from the local planning authority."

"Demolition was only cheaper by fifteen thousand pounds," she retorted. "A drop in the bucket for someone like you."

Barrett leaned in. "A new building would have wiped the slate clean. We could have still rebuilt and kept with the aesthetic of the area. It would have been far easier than going through the loopholes of renovating and making sure the building complied with modern requirements. You're focusing on windows and balconies while I'm focusing on the bottom line. Emotion has no place in decisions of this magnitude."

A shrill wind tore through the ruins, whipping leaves and debris about. Like a screaming ghost, Barrett thought with a glare at the broken tower.

"You've made your stance on emotions clear," Mina bit out. "Business and obligations must be dealt without pesky feelings, right?"

Her words punched him in the gut. He'd hurt her. Again.

She started to turn away.

Barrett grabbed her hand. "Business has nothing to do with the child. I can be emotionally available for our son or daughter."

Mina simply stared at him, mistrust evident on her face.

Barrett released her hand and stepped back, wrestling his anger under control before he spoke again. "Is that why you didn't tell me? Did you think me incapable of showing emotion toward our child?"

"You can be emotional, Barrett."

Mina's shoulders drooped. He didn't want her like this, downtrodden and sad. He wanted her to be angry, defiant. Hopelessness was much harder to stand. He wanted to comfort her, support her. The vulnerability in her curved shoulders and the droop of her head threatened his control.

"You told me you never wanted to see me

again." Her voice was flat, but he heard the pain beneath her words, felt the stinging cut of truth.

He had been so angry and hurt, because that night he'd let her in, connected with her. He hadn't given her the details. But he'd told her that town house had been important, that moving forward with it would have been righting a wrong and helping Sawyer Development step into a new era of business. She could have told him then that she had submitted her report.

But then he'd gone and done what his parents did just hours later. He'd said things out of anger, emotion.

He started to say more. His eyes dropped down to Mina's lips. More memories of that night—her soft smiles and the sweet kiss they had shared that had flared into something more, that sense of connection and belonging—tangled with a sudden need to touch her again.

He reached out, then slowly, ever so slowly, laid his fingers against her face.

It would have been so much easier had she yanked away. But instead, Mina leaned into his touch.

"Sabrina," he whispered.

Mina suddenly straightened, jerked back. "No." She shook her head. "I'm not doing this again."

Before he could press her, she turned and walked away.

Every bone in his body screamed for him to go

after her. She'd already walked away from him once today. He shouldn't let her walk away again. But unlike when he'd let her go on the cliffs, when he'd been in shock over her unexpected pregnancy, now letting her go was strategic.

He still didn't agree with her not telling him about the baby, and they would have to have that out eventually. But he could now acknowledge that he had hurt her—handled things badly in London, to say the least.

He wasn't sure what their relationship would look like moving forward. But he would be involved in his child's life. And he and Mina were going to have to figure out their own relationship as well.

He took one last look at the ruins of the North Wing.

His goal this morning had been to see Mina, prove to himself that his dreams and memories of her were far superior to reality, and then forget her as he focused on continuing to grow Sawyer Development.

But now he was going to be doing absolutely everything possible to keep Sabrina Callahan in his life.

CHAPTER SEVEN

Mina

Golden sun shone down on the land and sea, turning the yellow, orange, and red leaves still clinging to the trees into a fiery display of autumn color. The clouds had disappeared overnight, leaving behind a cool, earthy scent mixed with the salt from the ocean and wood smoke pouring out of the chimneys in town. The kind of day Mina usually loved.

But today, and she suspected for the rest of the week, she would be anything but calm.

She drummed her fingers once on the leather-bound cover of the diary in front of her. Her cousin had sent it to her from France, currently snuggled up with her former best friend and now fiancé.

Mina smiled slightly. Arlowe had been a whirlwind of sunshine, adventurous and supportive just seconds after they had met. Realizing she was a cousin had been an incredible blessing. She had even reached out to check on Mina last week, the text coming in just after Mina had returned from

Austria and learned that Barrett was coming to Glenvarra.

Since then, Arlowe had taken to checking on Mina almost daily. And this morning, she had sent a present.

Their late grandmother's diary.

Mina hadn't liked Desdemona's clause that she marry within a year. None of the cousins had, although Ivy Larken had been the loudest dissenter, vowing she would never get married regardless of the fortune their grandmother had dangled as an incentive. But Arlowe had included a brief note that said the diary answered some of their questions about their grandmother's obsession with marriage.

After reading of her grandmother's marriage to an older man who had claimed her unborn child as his own, a marriage that had miraculously turned into love, Mina understood more. She didn't agree with her grandmother's choice. But at least there had been a reason. For her grandmother, marriage had been a saving grace.

And she had been determined to see that her granddaughters didn't follow in their fathers' footsteps when they were handed their fortune. Unfortunately, it hadn't just been Mina's father who had chosen indulgence over responsibility. Both of her uncles had led similar lives. They had preferred money, alcohol, and women over responsibility.

She traced her fingers over the worn, softened

leather and her paternal grandmother's initials carved into the cover. It must have been hard for her to watch her sons fall one by one after all the happiness she'd experienced in the early years of her marriage. Perhaps she had felt the same kind of disappointment Mina had felt when she'd realized the kind of man her father had been.

Mina had always felt like there had been a piece of her missing. Her mother and maternal grandmother, *Mamó*, had told her so much about their side of the family history. She had fallen in love with the past because of them. *Mamó* especially had known everything about every building in town, down to what quarry the stones were mined in.

Yet always there had been that emptiness, that piece of her history that, no matter how many times she had asked, Mama and *Mamó* gently but firmly refused to disclose.

Her mother could have told her all the horrible things her father had done. She would have been well within her rights to slander the man to Dublin and back. Instead, she chose silence, not wanting to taint the identity Mina had crafted in her head. An identity that had started to unravel the night Mina overheard her mother crying to her grandmother, overheard bits of truth about the man her mother had once let herself love. A man who had abandoned Mina's mother when she needed him most.

Yet even then, there had been a part of her that had clung to the fantasy. A part of her that had wished her mother was wrong or bitter over her failed relationship.

So foolish.

Mina glanced toward the North Wing. That was at least one positive thing about Barrett. Unlike her father, he wasn't shying away.

Or negative, depending on how you look at it.

Yet here she was, angry at Barrett for offering what her father should have.

A frustrated sigh escaped her lips. She wasn't being fair. She had to reconcile that. She didn't care for the way Barrett had phrased things on the cliff yesterday. But a poor choice of words should not condemn her child to never knowing its father. She didn't need monetary support. But her child deserved to have a dad.

Well, Mina amended as she glanced down at her phone, *a dad who will be involved. Not just someone who will claim the title without putting in the work.*

She'd texted Thomas this morning asking him to meet her in the upstairs study. It had been over an hour, but she still hadn't heard from him. She couldn't imagine a scenario where he would say no. But he hadn't said yes yet, and that bothered her. She wanted to know he would follow through before she approached Bridget with her plan.

...you're going to enter into a coparenting relationship with the father of your child while marrying your best friend...

Even though things had been tense with Barrett yesterday, there was a tiny part of her that wished their relationship could be decent enough that he could fulfill the role of husband-for-a-year. Not that she envisioned them staying married past what the will required. But if she had to get married, it would be nice to marry the father of her child and break what felt like was becoming a generational curse for the Callahan women.

Callahan and Gruber, Mina amended, as she picked up the diary and flipped it open to the pages Arlowe had mentioned in her letter. The cursive was faint but elegant, spirals and loops dancing across the page even as her grandmother wrote of her deepest heartbreak. Desdemona had fallen in love at just eighteen with a man who was over a decade older than her. She'd been seduced and abandoned when she told her lover about her pregnancy.

Just a week before she became a bride, Desdemona had written:

> My father has found a husband who will take the baby and me. I'm saved from ruin. And my groom-to-be is surprisingly kind. Perhaps there are still one or two bright spots left.

Mina flipped ahead a dozen pages or so, a slight smile crossing her face as she came to a crinkled paper with penciled stars lining the edge.

> I have a son. A beautiful baby boy delivered just before midnight. And my husband, my dear sweet husband, held my baby in his arms and told me he was so grateful to be a father. I never thought I would fall in love again. But here I am, a wife and mother, and completely in love with the two most important men in my life.

Mina's heart sank as she slowly closed the diary. Her grandmother had been so happy. Happy to the point that she had given her sons everything, never wanting them to experience the fear, uncertainty, and humiliation she had in those first early months when she had been stranded and pregnant. Except she had spoiled her firstborn and the two sons that followed. Later passages included her regrets that she hadn't required her sons to do something responsible before she'd given them their trusts. Something like marriage.

A mistake, Desdemona had written in the final month of her life, she intended to rectify with her granddaughters.

Mina sighed. Even with a marriage in name only, the thought of wearing Thomas's ring on her finger while having Barrett's baby made her feel wrong, out of place.

"Interesting reading?"

Mina started even as Barrett's voice warmed her from the inside out. She closed the diary before turning to face him.

Stupidly handsome, again. White shirt, navy suit, and a black tie knotted to perfection. He stood in the doorway of the study, hands in his pockets and shoulders thrown back in his usual arrogant pose.

"Does it ever get exhausting?"

He arched a brow. "What?"

She gestured to the suit. "Suit, tie, not a hair out of place."

He shrugged. "Part of who I am."

She blinked. When she had walked by the night before the board meeting, his jacket had been draped over a chair, his tie nowhere to be seen, and his hair hanging loose as if he had run his fingers through it repeatedly. When he'd looked up at her, surprised and with his guard down, the attraction she had managed to suppress for months had broken through.

But now, seeing him once again buttoned up so tight, the sadness drove in deeper.

No, she didn't like the way he tried to barrel into her life after saying he never wanted to see her again. And she didn't like him becoming involved with the hotel. But she also didn't think Barrett was a bad guy. It was one of the reasons his cold fury in the aftermath of the board meeting had been so shocking. He struck her as someone who, at his core, was very lonely.

Barrett nodded at the diary. "What are you reading?"

She hesitated. A part of her wanted to share. Not about the marriage clause. He had been angry enough with her yesterday already. But she had told him during their night together how much not knowing her father had hurt her, had shared how diving into history helped fill some of that emptiness.

She mentally winced as she remembered telling him that homes had bones that always told a story. Some were more complete than others, but digging, learning, and figuring out how to renovate and reuse had been the fun part of her job.

And he had listened. That was always one of the challenges with Barrett. Even before that night, he had always listened and respected what she had to say, even when he disagreed. She had always spoken her mind. But with Barrett, she had felt safe, even emboldened.

But at the board meeting, it was like a different person had taken over. She had not recognized the man who turned down her ideas, who insisted so vehemently against renovation.

Torn, she glanced down at the diary. Then, with a deep breath, she made her choice.

"It's actually my grandmother's diary. My father's mom. She passed away." She paused, breathed in. "I learned my father's been dead for some time, too. Almost a decade."

Silence reigned. Barrett's eyes stayed fixed on her face. That intimate gaze should have made her feel stripped bare but instead provided an anchor as the emotional storm of the last few months whirled inside her.

"You don't know how to feel."

Surprised, she laughed quietly. "No, I don't. All these years wondering, missing, even sometimes hating him. And now…" Now there would be no stories. No conversations, no apologies.

"I'm sorry, Mina."

Her throat thickened. "Don't do that."

"What?"

She stood, grabbed the diary off the table, and clutched it to her chest. "Be nice."

"Why not?" he asked quietly.

"Because then I remember and I… I…"

He stepped forward. "You what, Mina?"

And then I want more.

She looked up, her eyes landing on his lips. They had almost kissed yesterday. Worse, she wanted to kiss him. Wanted to share the letters she'd written, tell him about the first ultrasound, the first time she'd felt the baby kick. She didn't just want the physical intimacy. No, she wanted something far more than Barrett would ever be able to give.

She shook her head. She needed to put a stop

to this. They had had one night, and they would only ever have that one night. She could not let herself fall any deeper. It hadn't just been embarrassment and rejection the morning he'd severed their relationship. It had been heartache for what she thought had been growing between them.

"There you are!"

Bridget walked in with a huge smile. Mina flinched as she forced a smile back.

"Hello, Bridget."

Bridget glanced between the two of them. "Glad to see you two together."

Mina tensed, but Barrett looked unaffected.

"Miss Callahan is a gifted storyteller." He glanced around the study. "She brought the history of the castle to life on our tour yesterday."

His compliment shouldn't mean anything. But it did.

"I remember the first time she came here for tea," Bridget said. She held up a picture. "In fact, look what I found. It was in one of the picture frames we rotated out of the grand hall over the summer."

Before Mina could reach out, Barrett took the photo from Bridget. The softening of his face was so small Mina would have missed it if she hadn't been watching him closely. He held the photo up. "Miss Callahan as a child, I'm assuming?"

"And her mother and grandmother," Bridget added.

Barrett stared at the photo a moment longer. "You have a beautiful family, Miss Callahan."

Most people would have missed the quiet envy in his tone. But whether it was because Mina knew Barrett better or simply because she recognized the feeling, she heard it. The envy and the sadness.

Slowly, Mina walked over and looked over his shoulder. The memory seeped in.

Her fifth birthday, complete with a rose-colored dress, braids in her hair, and a brand-new pair of white shoes with bows on top. The first time she had visited for more than a simple walkthrough to look at Christmas decorations. She'd sat at the table in the restaurant, her eyes getting bigger and bigger with every treat the waiter brought to their table. Every moment had felt so right. Like coming home.

They'd come back every year after. After her tenth birthday it was just her and Mama, but they had always ordered a third slice of cake for *Mamó*. They would take it home and eat it the following morning for breakfast.

Her lips curved into a smile. "I can't wait to do this with the baby."

The words were out before she could catch herself. She froze, not trusting herself to look at Barrett as she sensed his eyes on her.

"I won't keep you," Bridget said, oblivious to the sudden tension. "I was heading up to the third-floor storage when I saw you in here. Keep the photo, although I'd love to have a copy for the hotel, too." She turned to Barrett. "I have availability this afternoon, Mr. Sawyer, if you're still wanting to meet."

Panic flared. Was Barrett already pressuring Bridget to sign?

Mina glanced down at her phone, but the screen remained stubbornly blank. Where was Thomas? What if he was out on the property somewhere, caught up with a project? What if Mina wouldn't be able to talk to him until after Bridget's meeting with Barrett?

"Actually," Mina said as Bridget turned to the door, "I had a question for you. Do you have a moment?"

"Sure."

Mina started to follow Bridget out into the hallway.

"Miss Callahan."

Mina sucked in a breath and turned to face Barrett. "Yes, Mr. Sawyer?"

"Have dinner with me tonight."

She stared at him.

"Please," he added.

Aware of Bridget within earshot, Mina frantically scrambled for a reason to say no.

"Uh…"

"I really enjoyed your tour yesterday, and I was hoping to ask a few more questions." He raised his eyebrows slightly. "Before I make my decision."

Oh, you bastard. "Of course," she replied through gritted teeth.

"I'll pick you up—"

"No!"

She didn't want Barrett anywhere near her home. Picking her up would feel too much like a date. Besides, her cottage was right next to her mother's home. Seven would be right around the time her mother would be getting off shift from the hospital. What if her mother got home in time to see Barrett or, God forbid, ask to be introduced? And if she figured out who Barrett was? Mina was nowhere near prepared to have that conversation.

Barrett's eyes sharpened, but thankfully he didn't press. "I can meet you. Seven at the castle restaurant?"

When she nodded, he inclined his head. "Until then, Miss Callahan."

He walked past her, said goodbye to Bridget, and disappeared down the hallway.

Bridget slowly turned and shot Mina a smile. "Dinner, huh?"

"You did want us to spend time together."

"Still…"

"Bridget." Mina cut her off with a forced laugh. "I'm going to be a mom in a couple of months. I'm not interested in dating." She scoffed. "Certainly not a man like Mr. Sawyer."

Bridget frowned. "What's wrong with Mr. Sawyer?"

Mina hesitated. She needed to be professional and not let her personal feelings get in the way. Besides, she had just reminded herself, even though she didn't like the way Barrett did business, it didn't make him a bad person.

Just pushy, rude, and arrogant.

"When I worked for him," Mina finally said, "our views did not align."

"How so?"

"I like to preserve history. Mr. Sawyer prefers progress."

"Both have their place." Bridget glanced up at the dark wood beams crossing the ceiling of the study. "Although I do prefer preservation when possible."

"I do, too. Although," Mina said grudgingly, "I don't know if he told you, but when I took him on a tour of the North Wing, there was a crack in the east wall of the tower. It was mostly straight, but there were a few deviations."

"Mr. Sawyer mentioned it already, but I appreciate you letting me know, too. Our engineer from Dublin should be out later this week or early next to examine it."

Hopefully the engineer would take one look and deem the crack as normal movement for a structure of that size. No, Mina hadn't liked the look of it, but she hadn't liked Barrett's immediate fixation on the crack, either. She wouldn't put it past him to paint the worst-case scenario and use it as an excuse to demolish rather than renovate.

"About the North Wing, Bridget, would you be willing to consider another offer for financing the renovation?"

Wariness passed over Bridget's face. "What kind of offer?"

"Mine."

The wariness disappeared as Bridget gave her a sweet, indulgent smile. "Mina, I know you love the hotel. But I don't want you to take on a financial burden."

"It wouldn't be a burden. You know how I went to Austria for my grandmother's funeral a couple weeks ago? She left me money. A lot. You said the quote was nine million euros, and I'll have fifteen."

Bridget's eyes bugged. "Fifteen million?" she repeated in a stunned voice.

"Yes. I won't have access to the money for a year, but I can show you any paperwork you need, and surely we can find some way to use that as collateral to get started. I want the opportunity to finance the renovation."

Bridget's hand flew to her mouth. "Mina..."

"Please consider it, Bridget. I know Mr. Sawyer has a lot to offer. But I wouldn't ask for any ownership. And my primary focus would be restoration whenever it was possible."

Bridget stared at her for a long moment. "I'll

admit I have concerns about him having a share in the hotel. But his offer is generous. I like that he has a construction team, an architect, and engineers at his fingertips. He's also willing to invest in a project several others have turned down." She shook her head. "I couldn't believe it when he actually replied that he was interested."

Mina could feel Bridget starting to slip away before she had even begun. She didn't like not having Thomas's confirmation, but she'd track him down as soon as Bridget left. Get his answer, and if for whatever reason he declined, she'd simply find someone else.

A thought that left her nauseated. She could barely stomach the idea of marrying her best friend in name only. What if Thomas said no? What if she had to offer up three million euros to an acquaintance or even a stranger?

Mentally steeling herself, Mina plunged forward. Róisín was worth it.

"Let me put together an offer. Regardless of your decision," she added softly, "I'll be here as long as you want me."

Bridget reached out and wrapped her in a hug. "Mina, you are invaluable to Róisín."

Mina hugged Bridget back. No matter what happened over the next week, she would need to remember that she had developed something incredible here.

Bridget pulled back. "I'll have to tell Barrett there's another offer. But," she added, "I won't tell him who. Not yet, anyway. And I trust you to continue selling him on the hotel."

"I will."

Bridget looked down at Mina's stomach. "Your baby is incredibly lucky to have you as a mother."

Mina's eyes filled with tears. "Sorry." She wiped a couple teardrops off her cheek. "I'm a lot more prone to tears these days."

"I mean it, Mina. You have a sense of honor that is rare today. I know I can trust you to do the right thing."

Instead of warming her, Bridget's words turned Mina's blood cold. Was she acting honorably? Offering money before she secured a husband? Going behind Barrett's back?

She hadn't seen her submission of her report to the compliance officer as betraying him. He hadn't left her room to do her job, had refused to review her report or discuss it further.

But this…this was most definitely going behind his back.

"Thank you," she murmured faintly.

"Of course." Bridget arched her brows suggestively. "Now go home, get dressed up, and enjoy your dinner with a single handsome billionaire."

As Bridget walked away, Mina shook her head.

The last time she had dinner with a billionaire, she ended up pregnant.

Hopefully tonight's dinner would have a far less dramatic ending.

CHAPTER EIGHT

Barrett

THE LAST TIME Barrett had been this angry, he'd been watching one board member after another vote against demolishing the townhouse in Mayfair. Back then, it had been his proposal versus Mina's.

Now, it was his offer against another's, one whose identity Bridget hadn't shared. What she had told him, however, was that the new offer did not include any stipulation for controlling shares in the hotel.

He'd asked for the meeting to discuss the crack he observed during his tour of the North Wing. It had not, as he suspected, been in last year's engineering evaluation. The length and width of the crack appearing so quickly told him the costs for renovation were probably going to be higher than nine million.

To her credit, Bridget had immediately offered to have the engineering firm she worked with out for an evaluation. And then she'd dropped her bombshell of another offer.

Barrett picked up his wineglass and studied it in the light. He'd seen far too many businesses collapse after an influx of cash or rushed development. He wasn't going to let that happen, not on his watch.

Mina didn't understand why, and he didn't owe her an explanation. Whether or not telling her might have softened her impression of him was irrelevant. He needed to stay strong, impervious. That had been one of his two primary goals when he'd first come to Glenvarra: prove to himself that Mina was simply a woman he'd had a momentary attraction to, nothing more.

He glanced toward the doorway and froze.

Mina walked toward the table, dressed in a dark blue gown with billowing sleeves cinched at her wrists, the flowing skirt brushing the floor. Her red-gold curls had been twisted up into a bun, though several strands had escaped to frame her beautiful face.

He stood and pulled out her chair. "Good evening."

"Hello," she said softly.

"You look beautiful."

"Thank you." Her cheeks turned pink as she sat and glanced around, studiously avoiding his gaze. "Did you bribe one of the waiters?"

"Perhaps. Although it would be nice to know what you're accusing me of."

Mina nodded toward the massive arched windows overlooking the lantern-lit balcony and the harbor beyond. Boats bobbed gently on the dark water. "This is considered one of our best tables."

"No bribery." He shook his head. "I suspect Bridget requested this for us."

Mina's blush deepened. "Oh."

"Oh?" he echoed.

"Bridget suggested that you and I…" Mina's blush deepened. "That is, that we…"

"Does she suspect?"

"No." Mina glanced around, making sure no one had overheard. "No. She just thinks something could develop between us. I think she's trying to play matchmaker."

The idea of an actual romance with Mina should have been an immediate turnoff. Instead, Barrett found it all too easy to imagine reaching across the table, grabbing Mina's hand in his, and bringing it to his lips.

"We will have to talk about what the future will look like," he said.

Mina looked as if she'd rather take a jump off the cliffs. "I know."

"But for now, why don't you tell me what's good here?"

"Me?"

"This is your country, your home." He smiled. "I'm not familiar with Irish cuisine."

The smile that lit Mina's face filled him like nothing else had in a long time. "All right."

The waiter approached, and Mina ordered Dublin Bay prawns, potato gnocchi with brown butter and shaved cheddar, wild mushroom tartlets, and a glass of nonalcoholic red wine. But not before asking the waiter how his mother and sister were doing and how his schoolwork was going.

It came so naturally to her, this ability to draw out stories and make people feel seen. He both envied and admired it.

Once the waiter left, Barrett leaned back and took a sip of his wine. "How was your day?"

"We don't have to make small talk."

"Are you uncomfortable?"

"No, just—" She stopped. "Actually, yes. I am."

"Why?"

"That night…" Her voice trailed off. "I don't want to let you in."

His fingers tightened around his wineglass. A sentiment he understood all too well. But hearing it from her bothered him in a way it shouldn't have. "I see."

"That time we spent together, I… I really enjoyed it." Her cheeks warmed. "And the next day hurt. For a lot of reasons."

He slowly set his glass down. "I agree. I was blindsided in that board meeting."

"Barrett, if I'd had any idea that submitting my concerns to the risk officer would have gone to the board as quickly as it did or that they would add a last-minute vote to your meeting, I would have told you sooner."

"Were you planning on telling me at all?"

"I was." She said it with such conviction it was difficult not to believe her.

"Then why didn't you tell me that night?"

"Because…" She stared at the table. "Because I was enjoying my time with you. It was selfish, and I should have shared, but I thought I'd have more time."

…I was enjoying my time with you.

They'd sat cross-legged on his couch eating Chinese out of take-out cartons. There'd been no Michelin-star restaurant or expensive wine, no limo ride to or from dinner. It had been one of the simplest meals he'd had in a long time.

He believed that she had enjoyed her time with him. Not his wealth or his social standing but just him.

And he hadn't been able to just accept it. No, at the first sign of something suspicious, he'd pushed her out the door with both hands.

Mina's eyes flicked up, and she met his gaze head-on. "I wouldn't change what I did. You had every right to tell me no and insist we carry on with the demolition. But as the heritage consultant, it was my responsibility to submit those concerns. I followed corporate governance rules."

"You did," he admitted.

She had taken all the right steps. And he had made it difficult for her to share her opinion. But her not confiding in him after the intimacy they'd shared still stung.

Of course, he hadn't told her the real reason he wanted the building demolished. He hadn't told *anyone*. Perhaps if he had, the vote might have gone differently. But sharing what his father had done, what he had risked for a woman he had no intention of committing to beyond a few months, was something Barrett could not bring himself to do. Not now. Preferably not ever.

"I didn't like not knowing," he said quietly.

Mina nodded. "I can understand that. And I am sorry. It was not my intention to embarrass you or make you feel like I'd gone behind your back. I was trying to do what I thought was best for preservation. And technically, I didn't have to notify you at all."

It still hurt. But she had done nothing wrong. Whereas he had zeroed in on her, let his feelings about his father and the townhouse, and yes, his and Mina's night together take over. Ever since he had woken up that morning in his own bed and reached for Mina out of instinct, he'd been tense, irritated with himself. And when he'd walked into the board meeting and learned about the vote based on Mina's follow-up report, that tension had escalated into something uncontrolled and unreasonable.

Just like his parents.

His eyes dropped down to Mina's belly. Was he capable of being a good father? Or had he spent years trying to distance himself from his parents' legacy only to end up just like them?

No. His feelings toward Mina would need to be sorted through and dealt with. He needed to figure out how to be a partner while caring for their child while keeping the door closed on anything more.

But he would do everything in his power to be a good father.

"No, you didn't do anything wrong," he finally said. "I overreacted. I'm sorry."

Silence fell over the table. Mina bit down on her lower lip, confusion written across her face. "Thank you."

The waiter returned with their plates. Determined to regain control, Barrett steered the conversation back to the hotel. Between bites of gnocchi and sips of wine, Barrett peppered her with questions about Róisín. She answered each in classic Mina fashion with detail and stories that breathed life into the hotel. Everything she said supported Bridget's reports and the conversations he'd had with her. The hotel performed well financially, with opportunities to grow.

She paused her recitation to order duck confit

with cider-roasted apples for herself and seared monkfish with leeks for him. Color was high in her cheeks but not from embarrassment. No, Mina was excited. In her element. Her eyes were sparkling as she chatted with the waiter. And when she turned to look back at Barrett, a spontaneous smile on her face, his resolve shuddered.

She was beautiful, yes. But it wasn't just the curve of her jaw or the fullness of her lips that captured his attention. It was her, the easy conversation, listening to the melodic rise and fall of her voice.

"There's so much opportunity," Mina was saying as she plucked a mushroom tartlet off the plate.

"Bridget is favoring renovation?" he asked.

Part of the tartlet's crust crumbled and fell onto Mina's plate. She slowly loosened her grip on the pastry and set it down.

"Relax, Mina. I'm not against renovation when it's the best course of action." He held up a hand as she opened her mouth. "What's done is done. I'm talking about now. About the castle."

"Fair." Mina let out a breath. "I'm sorry. Yes, she would like to renovate as much as possible." She picked up the tartlet again and indulged in a generous bite before continuing. "Obviously, with the extent of the damage and how much time has passed, some projects will require demolish-and-rebuild."

"What would *you* do?"

"Me?"

"Yes. If you were overseeing the renovation—if you were in Bridget's shoes—what would you do?"

"Okay." She set down her fork and picked up her glass. "I'll tell you my ideas for the renovation if you tell me why you've been so tense all evening."

His lips quirked. "And here I thought I'd been doing a good job hiding it."

"What's wrong?" she asked softly.

The gentleness in her tone, paired with genuine concern, pulled him in. Mina didn't want to know because he was a billionaire or a CEO. She simply wanted to *know*.

"Bridget told me about the other offer today," he said. "I assume you know."

Mina blinked. "Yes."

"The other offer doesn't require any ownership stake."

Mina's lips parted, but she didn't say anything.

"What?" Barrett prompted.

"Why do you have to have an ownership in every project?"

Barrett set down his fork and took a long drink of wine. He wasn't used to sharing, especially anything connected to his father. But if he hoped to convince Mina he could be a good father and could open up to their child emotionally, now was a good time. He could share enough without letting her in too deeply. Besides, this was a new norm he was going to have to get used to if they were going to coparent successfully.

"My grandfather started Sawyer Development. When my father took over, he made bad decision after bad decision. He was fixated on emotion, on how a deal felt. He didn't do due diligence, and the company didn't have a board then. Not until later in his tenure, when he nearly ran the company into the ground with his spending."

"I didn't know that," Mina said softly.

Barrett looked out the window toward the cliffs. "It's rarely talked about. It took me years to move the company away from his reputation. He loved taking on small companies, throwing lavish money at extravagant renovations, reaping his benefits, then walking away and leaving them with structural issues or no cash flow." He faced Mina again. "He especially liked old things. That's how he and my mother met. An auction at Sotheby's. They both bid on a portrait by Sir Thomas Lawrence. My father won with a half-million-pound bid and gifted it to my mother. He didn't mention that he had bought the painting using my grandfather's account."

Understanding flickered in Mina's eyes. "I still don't know a lot about my father. But he did similar things to his mother, my grandmother, several times. Just learning about it hurt. I'm sorry you had to live with it."

Barrett understood now why Mina had told

him to stop earlier in the study, why she hadn't wanted his words. He knew in this moment she truly meant what she said, that she had some inkling of what he had lived through and genuinely hurt for him. It was unnerving.

"Thank you," he finally said. "One of the reasons my mother, and the mistresses that followed, fell for my father was because of his grand gestures. The same applied to his clients and the promises he would make for their properties and developments. He made money on the fees, then spent it on bigger projects. Many companies didn't understand what they were getting into. A lot went under."

Mina's eyes widened. "And that's why you require partial control."

"Yes. I help guide the business in the years after. I don't require it for smaller-scale projects or if the client has additional financial resources to support them if the worst were to happen. For those I do require a stake in, there's always a structured option for the owner to buy back my shares later. I never want anyone feeling beholden to me for life. But I won't let more businesses get run into the ground."

"That's admirable."

He smiled faintly. "Did it hurt to say that out loud?"

She chuckled. "A little."

"I know I can come across as cold," he said.

"But there are reasons for what I do. Now you owe me an answer. What would you do with the renovations?"

Mina hesitated, as if she wanted to press him further. He steeled himself. He'd already shared far more than he had intended. And her reaction had complicated things. What should have been a simple sharing of a reason for his business practices had left him wanting to tell Mina even more.

The exact opposite of what he should be feeling. God, what was it about Mina that kept drawing him in? And how was he going to control it?

Not by listening to her, he acknowledged a scant ten seconds later. Mina wasn't waxing poetic about the castle or its previous inhabitants, wasn't focusing on the pretty details his parents had preferred over important things like restoring a crumbling foundation to modern code. No, Mina's knowledge and experience were evident as she talked about using reclaimed stone and timber, incorporating historic fireplaces, matching window proportions, reinforcing walls with modern structural supports. She had no illusions, he realized, about what it was going to take to restore the North Wing. But she had a vision, one she made come alive.

That was what had drawn him in first, he realized with a start. When he first met Mina and shaken her hand, it had been like waking up after a long sleep. A dreamland where he'd gone through the motions and done what he needed to do. But when he and Mina talked, when they discussed and argued, he had felt alive for the first time in years.

A sensation that hadn't dimmed in the last seven months.

What the hell am I going to do?

"Sorry." Mina shot him a shy smile as she picked up her wineglass. "I used to dream about what that wing would look like restored. Bridget's been kind enough to let me do the evaluation from a heritage aspect."

"You have a great vision. What do you like to do outside of work?"

The sparkle in her eyes vanished. "Barrett—"

"I shared with you, Mina," he interrupted quietly. "Why are you so reluctant to tell me anything?"

"It's been twenty-four hours since you came back, and before that…seven months."

He usually prided himself on his patience. But with Mina, he felt none. "I know we're not going to immediately be best friends. But surely, knowing more about each other can't hurt. I just told you about my father."

"You did, and I appreciate it." She shook her head and placed her napkin on the table. "Look, I have to go. I'll pay my share on the way out."

Anger rushed through him. "I invited you. I'll pay."

She didn't stay to argue, proof of how badly she wanted to leave. She murmured a quiet "thank you" and walked toward the front of the restaurant.

Barrett watched her collect her coat and slip out through the glass door leading to the courtyard. He signaled to the waiter. "Excuse me. I'm ready to pay."

"Of course, sir. Let me just get the check—"

"This should cover it." Barrett placed several large bills into his hand.

"Sir, this is far too much."

"I overheard your conversation with Mina," Barrett replied as he stood. "Consider it a donation toward your college studies."

"Wow. Thank you, sir."

He had intended tonight's dinner to focus primarily on business while giving him and Mina a chance to spend time together. He'd forced himself to lower his guard and share intentionally. It had taken effort and left him with more questions than answers about his relationship with Mina. But damn it, he'd done it, and when her turn had come to share, she'd run away. Again.

He opened the door to the courtyard and braced himself against the cool night air. This time, however, he wasn't letting Mina get away.

CHAPTER NINE

Mina

PAVED WALKWAYS WOUND through the gardens. Several maple trees stretched up to the night sky, their branches still full of color. Ferns had been planted around the perimeter, while ivy and climbing roses in varying shades of red and pink clambered over the stone walls. Plume-topped grasses gently waved in the breeze from the far end of the courtyard that opened out onto the cliffs. In the center of the garden, a stone fountain splashed, surrounded by wrought iron chairs and tables.

In the spring and summer, the courtyard was almost always full. But tonight, thankfully, Mina had it all to herself.

She hadn't left tonight out of anger or sadness or fear. It had been pure guilt that drove her out of the restaurant.

Learning Barrett's reasons for wanting a controlling share in the business made sense with the man she had worked for. He liked to be in control, but it had always confused her how much effort and interest he seemed to have in the properties and businesses he worked with.

How was she supposed to keep her heart hard to a man who was trying to do the right thing by the clients? Worse still, he had apologized. Barrett Sawyer had actually apologized. And that apology had taken over her guilt about her offer to Bridget and sent it skyrocketing.

She'd left the study after her impromptu meeting with Bridget and tried to track down Thomas, only to learn he had called in sick to work. She'd tried calling and texting him several times before he'd finally replied that a friend of his in Galway had had an emergency and he'd taken an early train out to see him. He was at the hospital now, he'd texted, and he'd call as soon as he could.

She still felt like there was more he wasn't sharing, but how could she press him for an answer when his friend was in hospital? She texted back her hope that the friend would soon improve and not to worry about calling. They could chat when he returned to Glenvarra.

Now, not only did she still not have an answer, but she also didn't have the one person who knew the full extent of her increasingly dramatic situation.

She wanted to tell her mother, wanted to confide in her the way she did about almost everything else. But fear held her back.

Her mother had gone through her own share

of ups and downs over the last few months, from learning she was going to be a grandmother to finally sharing the secret of Mina's parentage. Even though she had been sad for Mina when she'd learned the baby's father wasn't going to be involved, she hadn't blamed Mina. Not once.

Would that change once she learned who the father of Mina's baby was?

Mina stopped by the fountain. The waterdrops fell in arcs into the pool, sparkling like diamonds in the light of the lanterns. Coins littered the bottom of the fountain. Wishes, hopes, dreams.

What Mina wouldn't give to have a simple wish. Instead, all she had was secrets. Too many secrets piling on top of one another. Less than a year ago, she'd prided herself on her honesty. Now, she just felt like a liar.

She had purposely concealed she was the person behind the other offer. Some would argue that was business. But it didn't feel right. Wasn't right, Mina corrected with a sigh. If she were in Barrett's shoes, she would feel deceived.

She breathed in the crisp night air, savored the coolness on her skin. Despite Barrett's revelation, she was still the right person to finance the renovation of the North Wing. Her views aligned more with Bridget's view for Róisín and allowed Bridget to retain full control. But Mina needed to tell Barrett that she was the one making the other offer.

A door creaked softly behind her. Awareness

crept down her spine. She knew without turning that Barrett had followed her into the courtyard. Part of her wanted him to go away, give her time to think through what she was going to say.

But that would just be delaying the inevitable. And, she reminded herself, what did it matter?

He would have a right to be frustrated, even angry. But she couldn't let it matter. Couldn't let herself care about what he thought about her. At the end of the day, it wouldn't matter whether Barrett liked her or flat-out despised her. As long as he treated their child well, that needed to be her only concern.

Slowly, she turned.

Barrett strode toward her, his face determined, his gait steady.

Regret twisted in her chest. There had been several moments tonight when the past had fallen away and she'd enjoyed herself. No pain, no regret, just her and Barrett. *Perhaps it's better this way*, she thought wistfully as he drew closer. *Sever the connection now before I fall too deep.*

"Mina, we have to talk about this—"

"It was me."

His steps slowed, and he stopped a few feet away, a frown on his face. "What?"

"I made the other offer."

His frown deepened. "What?"

"I'm going to inherit fifteen million from my

late grandmother's estate. I made Bridget an offer this afternoon to finance the renovation."

Barrett went still. His face smoothed over until there was no sign of any emotion. Alarm bells rang in Mina's head. She recognized his expression. It was the same blankness as when she stepped into his office for the last time just before he instructed her to close the door. Just before he'd let the mask fall, let her see the full depth of his anger just before he told her he never wanted to see her again.

She started to tremble but clasped her hands together and forced herself to stand still. She needed to face this.

"You despise me that much?"

"No." Mina shook her head. "No, I—"

He closed the distance between them in two long strides. "You torpedoed my development at Ellison Square, you failed to tell me we created a baby, and now you're trying to undermine this project." He leaned down, anger burning in his eyes. "So, it's not a matter of whether or not you hate me but just how much."

"I don't hate you!" she nearly shouted. After a quick look around the courtyard to confirm they were still alone, she leaned forward and dropped her voice to a fierce whisper. "You want to know why I was so hurt? It wasn't just that I enjoyed talking with you and having dinner and sharing what we did. Before that night, I respected you.

And then I saw that other side of you and it made me—"

She cut herself off before she said something she would regret. Before she made a complete and utter fool of herself.

Barrett's hands closed over her shoulders.

She kept her eyes trained on the fountain just over his shoulder, couldn't bear to look at him and see her worst fear lurking in his eyes.

"Made you what, Mina?"

Start to fall in love. "I liked you. A lot." Shame burned in her throat, so hot she barely choked out the next words. "And you looked at me like I was worthless." She wasn't worth a conversation to clarify what had happened with her report. Wasn't worth more than a single night. Wasn't worth staying for.

Just like she hadn't been worth it for her father.

The emptiness welled up inside her. Emptiness, she'd called it. The missing piece. But it was more than that. It was a wound so deep she wondered if she would ever be rid of it.

"You're not worthless, Mina." Barrett's hands tightened on her shoulders. "I told you I made a mistake that morning. I should have talked to you."

She shook her head. "I'm not looking for another apology. I'm just trying to explain." Slowly, she raised her gaze to his. "I wasn't trying to hurt you, Barrett."

Silence fell once more between them. Somewhere in a nearby field a sheep bleated. From this high up, the waves crashing against the cliffs were a soothing shushing. The muted strains of music from the restaurant filtered into the courtyard.

Above it all, Mina's heart started to pound as Barrett's eyes gleamed in the darkness.

Don't give in. Stay strong.

"Say my name again," he murmured.

"What?"

"It's the first time you've said it in over half a year. Say my name again."

She shouldn't.

"Say it, Sabrina."

The earth shifted. She remembered him saying her name just like that, his voice husky and strained as if he could barely control himself. They'd stood by the window, warmth and tenderness and longing on his face just before he'd kissed her.

Just like now.

"Barrett."

And then she rose up and pressed her mouth to his.

CHAPTER TEN

Barrett

Barrett's arms flew around Mina as he pulled her close.

Too long. It's been too long.

He brought one hand up and cupped her face as he deepened the kiss. It wasn't just wanting her. It hadn't been seven months ago, and it wasn't now. Kissing Mina felt like coming home.

His other hand drifted down to her side and cradled the side of her stomach. The change in her body, knowing she carried their child, hit him with a raw need to pull her closer.

She moaned, the sound filling him as he deepened the kiss.

And then, just as quickly as it had started, Mina wrenched her head back. "We can't do this."

It took every ounce of self-control to release Mina and honor her request, even though it nearly killed him to let her go.

Mina placed a finger on her swollen lips, then snatched it away as if she been burned. "We need to figure something out about the baby. But you and I will never be good for each other."

Her words stung. But physical passion aside, she was right. While they'd never discussed it in detail, Mina had mentioned once she had wanted to get married and have a family. She might have skipped the first step for now, but eventually she would probably return to that dream.

A possibility that had his fingers curling into fists at his sides.

Her dating life was none of his concern. He would never be able to cede control to another person, let down his walls enough to love someone the way they deserved to be loved in a marriage. Emotions aside, there were logistics to be considered. He lived in London. She had settled back in Ireland. Coparenting a child across that distance was going to be challenging enough, let alone maintaining a relationship they both agreed wasn't the right choice for them.

Mina was making it easy. She wasn't asking for a ring or pressuring him for something he couldn't give. So why was it so hard to agree with her? Why did the words stick in his throat?

"We are very different," he finally said.

Some emotion crossed her face, but he couldn't discern what it was. "Yes." She shook her head. "About the deal…"

Right. The offer she made behind his back. Except she'd only made that offer this afternoon.

Probably, he realized, shortly after he left the study. And she told him several hours later. Besides, he had he never talked to a competitor about a deal beforehand. Expecting her to declare her business plans was unfair. He wouldn't expect it from any other competitor. But then, he had never wanted a personal relationship with a competitor before. "I am sorry." Mina sighed. "Unlike the town house, I wasn't going to tell you."

"But you did."

"I did."

He waited a moment, then decided to jump in. "Why didn't you come to me about the baby?"

Her smile was sad. "Part of it was pride. And for that reason, it was wrong. You said you never wanted to see me again. I found happiness here again. I love my job. I wasn't sure…"

Her voice trailed off, but the implication was clear.

"You thought I might try to hurt your career."

"I never would have thought that until we met after the board meeting. It didn't seem like you, but…"

But he hadn't acted like himself. Hadn't been cold and calm or professional. He'd let anger take over and dictate his actions.

He started to reach for her but forced himself to put his arm back down.

"Whenever I tried to convince myself that you were in shock because of the board vote, I remembered you saying that you never wanted to marry, that you never wanted children.

"And I know you like to date..." Her voice cracked. "Obviously what we had was just one night. But your reaction the next morning reinforced that you wanted a different kind of life, one the baby and I wouldn't fit into."

He'd hurt her. Far deeper than he'd realized. "I'm very sorry, Mina."

She slowly nodded. "I am, too."

"It's been a long evening. How about I walk you to your car?"

Her eyes narrowed with suspicion. "Just like that?"

"I want to discuss the details of how I'm going to be involved and what coparenting is going to look like. And yes, I'm going to convince Bridget to choose my offer over yours."

Mina snorted. "Good luck."

"But," he added as he looked deep into her eyes, "what I don't want to do is hurt you again. I don't know what coparenting is going to look like moving forward. But I do know I want our child to see his or her mother treated with the respect she's due. And I don't want to cause you that kind of pain ever again."

Mina stared at him with wide eyes.

He wanted to pull her into his arms, cradle her head against his chest as he told her over and over how sorry he was. But he didn't want to make another decision rooted in emotion when the last two times he succumbed to such feelings had resulted in a baby and pain to a woman who would become a target for his displaced anger.

"Okay." Mina nodded toward the castle. "Walking me to my car won't be necessary. I have an early morning event, so Bridget's letting me stay overnight."

"Then I bid you good night, Miss Callahan." Barrett inclined his head.

For the first time since arriving in Glenvarra, he was the first to walk away.

Mina

Mina glanced at her watch and mentally cursed. She had less than an hour before her appointment. The hospital was twenty kilometers away. If she left now, she would barely make it on time.

The stress of the last few days had taken its toll. Fortunately, most of the staff were dismissing her little mistakes here and there as pregnancy brain. But she was forgetting important things, too, like her prenatal appointment until a reminder had popped up on her calendar.

Given that she'd barely slept last night, it was understandable. But she didn't like it, just like she didn't like the memory of Barrett's kiss playing over and over through her head every time she closed her eyes.

She'd tossed and turned all night. She managed

to roll out of bed this morning, suffer through a historical breakfast with a Canadian tour group that included traditional dishes cooked in seventeenth-century Ireland and a tour of the castle's kitchens. She'd done a review of her checklist items for the Autumn Heritage Banquet and forced down soup and a piece of toast for lunch.

And she'd only thought about Barrett half a dozen times.

She'd done the right thing stopping that kiss, no matter how strongly she had wanted to surrender. The last time she did that, she'd ended up with a broken heart that had required considerable mending. Pulling away from Barrett and reestablishing boundaries had been the right thing to do.

Even if the words had tasted like ash in her mouth.

Enough. Right now, she needed to switch focus from work to the baby. Thankfully, when her calendar alert had popped up earlier that morning with the reminder about her doctor's appointment, her event team had stepped in to continue preparations for the banquet.

Mina pulled on her cloak and hurried out, waving but not stopping to talk to the attendant at the front desk on her way out. The drive alone took nearly thirty minutes, and that didn't include finding a parking spot, going inside and navigating the labyrinth of hallways that would take her up to the doctor's office.

She tried and failed not to glance around to see if Barrett was around. Fortunately, she hadn't seen or heard from him all morning. *Fortunate*, she reminded herself firmly as she unlocked her car.

It had stung when he had pulled away last night, agreeing that resuming any physical intimacy was a bad idea.

Ridiculous. She had been the first to voice it. She had no right to be hurt when he'd acquiesced, doing them both a favor.

She opened the car door, wincing at the metallic groan that was emitted. She needed to get a new car. Part of her reluctance was nostalgia. This was the first and only car she had purchased after years of saving. And part of it was she didn't want to act like her father and blow her inheritance.

The thought of her father sent an unexpected surge of pain through her. Far more pain than she felt when she learned he'd been dead for ten years. She'd chalked up her lack of reaction to shock, a defense mechanism after decades of wondering. It was also hard to summon any sentimentality for the man who had turned his back on the mother of his child and wasted his fortune.

Her fingers tightened around the steering wheel. Even though she'd overheard that conversation between Mama and *Mamó* so many years ago, there had always been a part of her that hoped one day she might learn why. That there would be some crazy explanation that would make it all right.

The idea of a father had been far better than the real thing turned out to be.

Jakob Gruber had been a bastard. That didn't stop the pain from reappearing at random times. She would never know her father. Her child would never know its grandfather. The worst part was even if her father had lived, he most likely wouldn't have cared to meet either of them.

And now she was on the verge of following in her mother's footsteps, falling for a man who would never be able to care for her the way she cared for him.

She was afraid for her child, too. Yet no matter how many times she examined the subject, she always came up with the same answer.

Barrett would not make the same mistakes her father had. At his core, he was an honorable man. He would do the right thing, even if he didn't want to.

But she didn't want to be an obligation. She needed to keep her walls up around her heart. It was going to be hard balancing letting him into her child's life while keeping him out of hers. But that was her problem, not his, not their child's.

She shoved the key into the ignition a little harder than she should have, then turned it. Nothing. Not even a sputter.

"You've got to be kidding me." She pulled the key out, reinserted it, tried again. This time there was the tiniest cough, followed by another long silence.

Mina dropped her head onto the wheel.

Mama was at home, her first day off in nearly a week. Thomas was still in Galway, Bridget was meeting with her accountant, and every other person she could think of was working. She could find a taxi, but it wouldn't be cheap, and until she was officially married, she was trying not to touch the initial twenty-five-thousand she had received from her grandmother's estate. Once she started dipping into that, it was only a matter of time before she started using it more and more. She needed that safety net for her and her baby if and when they needed it.

A knock on the window made her jump. Her head snapped, and she was too tired to stop herself from rolling her eyes.

Barrett.

Of course, Barrett was here.

Reluctantly, she opened the door.

"If you can afford to renovate a historic castle, surely you can afford to buy a car made in this century."

She tapped her fingers against the steering wheel. "I've had other things on my mind. Now if you'll excuse me, I'm having a good moan."

He arched one brow. "A moan?"

"A sulk. Feeling sorry for oneself."

"My apologies," he said, his dry tone implying that he wasn't in the least bit sorry. "Need a lift?"

"No." She pulled her phone out of her coat pocket. "I'll get a taxi."

"Glenvarra has taxis?"

"Yes and…" Her voice trailed off at the estimated wait time on the app. Over an hour. The doctor's office would work with her some, but surely not that much.

"Problem?"

She sighed. She didn't want to reschedule. Everything was going well so far, but she didn't want to risk missing something. And the banquet was this weekend. She wanted to know everything was all right before she spent the majority of Friday and Saturday on her feet.

Reminding herself it was for the baby, she gritted her teeth and faced Barrett. "Yes. I could use a ride. Please."

Barrett nodded, his face blank. "Sure, where to?"

"The hospital in Drogheda."

His eyes widened. "Hospital?" He opened the door wider and crouched down. "What's wrong?" He reached out and cupped her face. "Are you having contractions? Are you in pain?"

Shaken, Mina just sat there. "I'm okay. And so is the baby," she added. "It's just a routine appointment."

He breathed in, then out. "You're sure?"

"I am."

Slowly, he nodded. "Okay. Obviously, I don't have a lot of experience with this, and when I hear the word *hospital*, I think emergency."

"Understandable. I'm sorry. I should have said the doctor's office. It's at the hospital where I..." She paused for a moment. "Where we'll have the baby."

Barrett stared at her for a long moment. His hand gentled on her cheek, his fingers trailing delicately over her skin before he stood and held out his hand to her. "Thank you, Mina."

She stared at the outstretched fingers. This was momentous. Not just her acknowledgment of him being present for the baby's birth, but her accepting his help, letting him take her to this appointment. It was the first step toward inviting Barrett to be an involved father.

Slowly, she reached out and placed her hand in his.

CHAPTER ELEVEN

Mina

THE CAR SPED down the road, passing farms dotted with sheep and orchards heavy with apples, pears, and plums. Blackberries grew thick on the hedgerows as a beautiful blue sky stretched overhead. It was the same drive she'd been taking off and on for the past five months, ever since she found out she was pregnant. But now, from the passenger seat in Barrett's car, Mina had the luxury of being able to simply enjoy the scenery.

It certainly helped that Barrett's car, like pretty much everything else he owned, was top of the line. Buttery leather seats warmed to perfection, recessed lighting that instantly relaxed her, and a touch screen panel with an overwhelming amount of customizable options.

"How's the planning for the banquet going?"

Okay, he was trying to be pleasant. She could handle small talk. Besides, even though she wanted him to take his offer and hightail it back to London as soon as possible, she had made a promise to Bridget.

"Well. Everything's actually lining up really well."

"How'd you come up with this event?"

She glanced at Barrett out of the corner of her eye, but his gaze stayed focused on the road.

"Bridget and I had been talking about hosting a gala. An event where people could get dressed up, have fun at a glamorous banquet. The more we talked, the more we realized how much an event like that could not only be fun but benefit the town and the surrounding businesses."

"And give Róisín free marketing."

"What's wrong with that?"

"Nothing. It's clever. I've been impressed with what I've seen before."

Mina gritted her teeth. She was doing her job and honoring her pledge to Bridget.

"Did you ever think you would go into event planning?"

"No. But when I came back to Glenvarra, it was the only job available at Róisín. Fortunately, Bridget gave me plenty of leeway to develop the position and make it into what it is now."

"Do you miss what you did in London?"

Another side glance revealed nothing. "Yes and no. I miss getting to see all the different properties. But I don't miss the bureaucracy or the paperwork."

Or navigating an administrative minefield.

"You thought I was angry with you because you disagreed with me."

Startled, Mina turned her head. "About the town house?"

"Yes."

Slowly, she nodded. "Yes. Honestly, it surprised me. We had always been able to talk, and even when we disagreed, I felt like we could still communicate about it. But, when you shut me down in the staff meeting, before I could share my concerns, I didn't know what else to do but prepare my own proposal." She turned and stared out at the winding road in front of them. "I know it was close on cost. But for a few thousand pounds' difference, not to mention the potential risk that would come from demolishing a building with so much historic significance, I didn't understand why you were so fixated on tearing it down."

"It had nothing to do with cost or preservation. It had everything to do with my father."

Mina glanced at him. "Your father?"

He nodded, his hands tight on the wheel and his lips thin.

She looked away, sensing he was about to tell her something he had never shared with anyone else.

"My father acquired that town house. It was back in his early days. It was set to be condemned, so he got it for a steal. He said it was for an investment. He bought it for one of his mistresses."

Mina's heart dropped. She could hear the pain lingering in Barrett's voice, the same pain she'd felt when she overheard her mother crying to her grandmother and realized the extent of how cruel her own father had truly been.

"He took his mistress to the town house one night, showed her around. She became obsessed with saving it." Barrett shook his head. "Obviously, as you know, it can be saved. But my father wasn't interested in foundational or structural concerns. He simply wanted to make it pretty, bring it to life the way it had looked all those years ago. So, he used company money under the guise of doing up a few rooms to show what the town house could be as an investment for a hotel, private residence, I forget all of the things he included."

He stopped for a moment, cleared his throat, and continued to speak.

"My mother wasn't a saint, either. She was like a lot of his mistresses, with big dreams and big ideas and not enough common sense to support them. Selfish, argumentative, and she had plenty of her own affairs.

"But Dad was behaving differently this time. Spending more money than he usually did, mentioning to Mom how young his mistress was, how maybe they should finally call it quits."

"Your mother didn't want a divorce?"

"In her own way, she loved my father. I think they both enjoyed the drama of their marriage and liked indulging with other lovers when it suited them. But she thought they would always come back to each other.

"One night, three or four months after the affair started, she came to me. It was the first time she had sought me out since I went to university."

"The first time?" Mina repeated softly. When Barrett nodded, she reached over and laid a gentle hand on his shoulder. "I'm sorry, Barrett. You deserved better than that."

His jaw tightened. "It's in the past."

Except it wasn't. The pain still lurked in the tightness around his eyes and the muscles coiled beneath her fingers.

But she let it drop, removed her hand and settled back into her seat.

"Dad had stopped by her penthouse and asked if she would consider an uncontested divorce. He wanted it over as quickly as possible so he could marry his mistress. She wanted to start a family."

Barrett glanced over as Mina's jaw dropped. His smirk was humorless, bitter.

"He didn't know the first thing about being a father. But he was ready to bring an innocent child into this world on a whim. Mom was hurt. I was furious. I..."

"You wanted to do something for her," Mina finally said softly.

Barrett grunted. "Foolish, but yes. I thought maybe it could turn out to be a fresh start. I just needed to convince Dad to drop his mistress and all his talk about divorce. I knew that he'd been working on the town house, but I thought it was just a few rooms. But when I walked in, I realized he'd been using company funds to turn it into his own little love nest. He hadn't just hurt my mother or turned his back on his only son so he could start over with a woman who was just a couple years older than me. He had risked the reputation of the company his own father built from the ground up, all so he could please a woman who was with him for his money."

The venom in his voice coated every word. Yet what other choice did Barrett have but anger? How many times had she indulged in anger to keep her own hurt at bay?

"I wanted to kill him."

Mina looked over at the same moment Barrett did, his eyes bleak.

"I don't mean that figuratively." He looked back at the road. "I truly did."

She reached over and laid her hand on his shoulder again. "I can understand that. But you didn't."

"I wanted to. Not just for my mother, either, but for myself. I spent so many years putting up a wall between myself and them. But that wall had holes in it. Holes that let pain still creep through. I learned that night standing in the entryway of that damned town house that I mattered less to him than a Rysbrack sculpture or a gilt bronze chandelier." He swallowed and finished his confession. "That pain made me desire the death of another human being. My own father."

Two more farms and a large meadow passed by before he spoke again.

"I don't know if you still want me involved with the baby after hearing that."

"We all have desires to do things we shouldn't want to. What matters are the choices we actually make." Her fingers tightened on his shoulder. "I personally have a lot more respect for people who are tempted to do the wrong thing and instead choose to do the right. Especially when there's a foundation for why they feel the way they do."

Silence reigned for several long seconds. Then, slowly, Barrett nodded. "Thank you."

She let go of his shoulder and threaded her fingers together to stop them from trembling. Part of her didn't want to hear any more. It just made it all that harder to keep him at a distance. But she owed him this. And she wanted to know, wanted to find out why he had been so furious with her that morning.

"I confronted him. Pointed out how what he had done was not only unethical but illegal. We fought. He told me aside from my mother I was the worst mistake he'd ever made."

Mina gasped. "Barrett."

He shrugged. "I'd always suspected it. I was so angry in the moment it didn't even really faze me. If anything, it made it easier to withdraw completely."

Just like his words to her that morning had made it easier for her to pull back.

"I took my concerns about the money and the renovations to some of the higher-ups, but so many of them were afraid of losing their jobs. A week later, my father hired somebody to come and install new windows. The ladder the installer used hit a weak spot in the floor just right. The beams underneath had been eaten through by termites. The man ended up in the hospital with multiple broken bones and a concussion. He survived, but he was never able to work in his field again."

"And that's why you instituted the board," Mina murmured softly as the puzzle pieces slid into place.

"I told my father to either implement a board or I would go to the media. He settled with the man out of court, and most of it was swept under the rug. My father sold off all the antiques he'd bought for the town house and two of his own cars to pay back the money he'd siphoned off. His mistress left him the day after the board gave him a vote of no confidence and nominated me as CEO. The last time I saw him, security was escorting him out."

"And your mother?"

Barrett's lips twisted. "She filed for divorce. Took everything she could and left the country. She married a Frenchman, divorced, moved to Australia and moved again. Last I knew, she was in Brazil with her fourth. It may be five by now."

Barrett shrugged as if it no longer hurt, even if she could still hear traces of anger and disappointment in his words.

One of the unexpected graces, Mina realized, of never meeting her father. She had been spared the incredible pain Barrett had been subjugated to over and over again by the very people who should have done everything they could to protect him.

Admiration kindled in her chest. Admiration and a different kind of warmth. Barrett had trusted her with something precious, something she never would have imagined he would have shared with her.

"For the longest time I didn't want to deal with the town house. Part of me just wanted to let it sit there and rot until there was no choice but to demolish it Then I could move on." His lips quirked up. "Until you came along and started reviewing our properties. I saw Ellison Square on your list and decided to move forward with the proposal for demolition. I just wanted it gone. A blight on the history of our company."

"You still stood up to your father. And when that didn't work, you tried to go to the people who should have fixed things."

"You went through the proper channels, too. And I condemned you for it. I don't know if I can fully express how truly sorry I am for that."

He reached over, laid his hand over hers. The physical contact sent electricity racing up her arm even as his apology softened her resolve to keep him out of her heart.

"I let my emotions take over. I wanted to get rid of a building I saw as both my father's failure and my own." He squeezed her hand. A gentle pressure, and then it was gone.

It took her a minute to gather her thoughts, to find her voice without sounding teary. "Thank you for telling me. And for your apology. I had no idea my inquiry to the risk officer would move so quickly. I just turned in the paperwork that morning."

"It was a good report. Whether I liked it or not, your argument was valid. The lawyer knew the board was meeting the next day and decided to escalate it. You didn't do anything wrong, Mina. I did."

They both fell silent for several kilometers. A small cemetery appeared surrounded by a low stone wall. Gravestones stretched up to the sky, from worn, cockeyed markers to newer-looking marble tombstones.

"I'm sorry about your grandmother. And your father," Barrett said as they drove past.

"Thank you. There's been some good at least. Not just the money, but I found out I have two cousins." Mina looked down at her hands. "All three of our fathers are dead."

"I'm sorry."

"I am, too." She watched the cemetery pass by and continued to stare out the window. "I honestly expected to have more of a reaction."

"Understandable why you wouldn't."

"Thank you." She paused. "I told you I overheard my mom and grandmother talking about him and I figured out he wasn't a nice person. But I didn't mention that I learned he left her when she told him she was pregnant. When I found out, all these years later, that he had been so wealthy..." She shook her head. "My mother is such an incredible woman. I hate that I still fixated on his identity after learning what a horrible person he was." Her voice dropped, "I even wondered if he might have liked me, just a little, if he had known me." She took a deep breath. "I feel so disloyal. My mother deserved better from me."

"It's natural to want to know, Mina."

She glanced over. "It means a lot that you shared your story with me, Barrett."

Out of the corner of her eye she saw the sudden tensing, his shoulders tightening as a muscle ticked in his jaw. "I wanted you to be aware of my background before we discuss our parenting agreement."

Before she could say anything else, he reached over and tapped the panel. A moment later soft notes of fiddles, flutes, and accordions filled the car.

Shocked by his abrupt withdrawal, Mina leaned back into her seat and closed her eyes. God, she was an idiot. Had she really thought she and Barrett were reconnecting? That everything he shared was a continuation of what had started that night in his office? There had been strategy to his divulgence.

Always strategy, she thought bitterly. He'd apologized, which was better than nothing.

But he had only confided in her to lay the foundation for being involved in their child's life.

She had been foolish to let down her guard so easily.

The words her mother had whispered to her just before she flew to Austria for the will reading came back to her.

Be strong, Sabrina. Depend on yourself first. Always.

The car sped on toward Drogheda.

CHAPTER TWELVE

Barrett

BARRETT PULLED INTO the hospital parking lot. The last ten minutes had been awkwardly silent, a silence he had caused.

He hadn't meant to be so abrupt when Mina thanked him. But hearing the warmth in her voice had stoked something inside him. The same need he'd once given into when he listened to his mother's tearful pleas and went to the town house to confront his father. The same wish he'd once murmured as he climbed the steps, that this time his father might listen to him.

The same cautious hope he'd experienced when he kissed Mina just before she left his office, her hair rumpled and her eyes glowing.

That sense of knowing, of recognition, had been even stronger that night. The longer they talked, the more he had relented. Let her in far deeper than he had anyone else in years. He'd invited her into his office, and even though he'd stuck to mundane topics, like why he'd gotten into property development and where he'd gone to university, Mina had listened, as she always did, with an intimate attentiveness that made him feel stripped raw and laid bare.

In the dark of night, letting down his guard and surrendering to a woman who had bewitched him with her confidence and caring had felt liberating. But in the light of day, as the president of the board presented him with Mina's report, he'd cursed himself for a fool. He had never wanted to be vulnerable with anyone again. His anger at his own choices had made him far more unreasonable with Mina than he had had a right to be.

Just like he was now.

He had owed Mina that explanation. She deserved to know why he'd been so angry, especially since it was one of the roadblocks to him being involved in their child's life. He understood and respected Mina wanting to protect their child.

But then, just when things had finally started to improve between them, he'd shut them down again. All because the balancing act of being with Mina without endangering his heart was more difficult than he'd anticipated.

Mina reached for the door handle.

He tried to think of something, anything, to break the tension.

And then she slowly looked over at him, her eyes big and blue and vulnerable. "Would you like to come in?"

His chest tightened. He didn't deserve her grace. He almost said no.

But then her hand drifted down to her stomach. That moment in the courtyard, when his hand had settled on her waist, and he'd felt the roundness of life growing beneath his fingertips, rose above the inner turmoil.

"I would."

She released a shuddering breath and nodded, as if reassuring herself she'd made the right choice in offering to let him come up.

"Wait." He got out and quickly circled the car, opening the door and extending his hand.

She didn't hesitate as long this time before taking it. His fingers wrapped around hers a little more tightly than he anticipated.

They only had two months of this. Two more months of her being pregnant. Whatever life looked like after that, he wanted to take advantage of every moment like this with her that he could, especially since he had missed the last seven months. Even if they weren't going to be romantically involved, he could still be a supportive partner.

You just want to touch her again.

He ignored the voice as Mina pulled her hand from his. But they stayed side by side as they walked into the hospital together.

One elevator ride, one long walk through a

maze of hallways, and one brief wait in the waiting room later, they were ushered into an exam room.

"Welcome." The nurse beamed at them. "Are you family?"

Barrett glanced at Mina.

"He's the father."

Warmth flowed through him. It was the first time Mina had referred to him as the father in front of anyone. A gift, he knew, that had most likely cost her.

The nurse brightened. "Oh! Well, we are so happy to see you. Mina is one of our favorite patients."

A delicate blush crept into Mina's cheeks. "She says that about all her patients."

The nurse snorted. "I most definitely do not." She arched a brow at Barrett. "Glad you were finally able to make it."

"Me, too."

The nurse set about taking Mina's vitals and asking her a few questions. Toward the end, a knock sounded on the door, and the doctor walked in.

"Mina." She turned and inclined her head toward Barrett. "And…?"

"Barrett Sawyer," Mina said. "The father."

The doctor smiled. "I'm glad to see you here. So, let's check the heartbeat."

The nurse helped Mina ease back on the examination table and lifted her shirt to reveal her pregnant belly. As Barrett watched, her skin shifted as something pressed from within.

"Is that…?"

The nurse chuckled and tapped her fingers against the bump. The bump grew larger. "I'm guessing a hand. You certainly have an active one."

Barrett stared a moment longer before his eyes shifted to Mina's face.

Her smile took his breath away, wide and glowing as she stared down at her belly. "She seems to like doing most of her movement in the middle of the night."

"She?" he repeated. "I thought you said you were waiting until the birth."

"I am. My mom thinks it's a boy, and she's usually right." Mina shrugged. "But ever since I found out, I've had a feeling it was a girl. It'll be fun to find out."

Barrett had never thought about what it would be like to find out if he was having a son or a daughter. But as the doctor spread clear gel on Mina's stomach, anticipation buzzed through him. Excitement, nervousness, a touch of dread. He didn't know the first thing about babies, let alone being a father.

But he wasn't going anywhere. And as he watched Mina's hand settle on the side of her stomach, he knew without a doubt she would teach him.

He blinked. He trusted her. Trusted her to love their child, to treat him as an equal and as a partner even though having him involved was the last thing she had wanted.

Shaken, he watched as the nurse murmured something to Mina. Watched as laughter lit her eyes. And felt his resolve to keep her at arm's length tremble.

"All right, let's find that heartbeat."

The doctor pressed a small wand against Mina's stomach. Barrett stood and walked closer. For a moment, there was nothing but a whooshing sound.

And then he heard it. Soft at first, then stronger, a growing gallop as their child's heartbeat filled the room.

He had traveled all over the world, met with some of the wealthiest people alive, spearheaded the development of some of the most incredible buildings in London. Nothing compared to this moment.

"Is that normal?" He looked at the doctor. "That sounds fast."

"One-forty," the doctor said with a small smile. "Perfect."

Warm fingers wrapped around his. Barrett looked down to see Mina's hand curled around his, just the way he'd held her hand when she got out of the car. Slowly, he looked up at her.

She was watching him with the softest light in

her eyes. No anger. No fear or suspicion. Just pure joy in sharing this moment with him.

His heart surged in his chest. He wasn't the right man for her. But when she looked at him like that, he wasn't sure how he was supposed to stay away.

CHAPTER THIRTEEN

Mina

MINA WALKED THROUGH the banquet hall, eyes skimming over every inch. Tables had already been set up, chairs put in place. Right now they were bare, but in three days, they would be draped in rich burgundy tablecloths. The guest tables would feature vases of flowers from a local florist and votive candles. Each place setting would have a small card with a historical fact about the castle or a brief biography of someone who had lived there.

It was the little touches Mina enjoyed the most. Loved giving the voices of the past one more night to shine, to let their stories be heard.

Framed photos of the castle's past tenants were scattered around the hall, the Grand Ballroom, the library, anywhere they anticipated guests.

Letters and old diary pages, with their faded writing preserved beneath glass, were interspersed with the black and white photos.

Mina had taken special care to select documents

written in the autumn months, from invitations to love letters to poetry.

But this morning, even as she made a mental note to shift the musicians to give the guests more room to dance, she couldn't keep Barrett from her thoughts. Again.

Hard to do when he had not only accompanied her to the appointment but also reacted the way he had, as if he were genuinely excited to become a father. The look of wonder on his face when he first heard the heartbeat, the warmth when he looked at her after she grasped his hand...

Heat pricked her eyes. Was this what the next two months were going to be like? Constantly trying to keep her walls up even as Barrett unintentionally chipped away at them?

Their ride back to Glenvarra had been quiet. But unlike the tension of the drive out, the silence between them had felt comfortable, familiar. And when Barrett had dropped her off at the castle, he came around and opened her door just like he had before. When she took his hand and let him help her out of the car, he had pressed a kiss to the back of her hand. *Thank you.*

Her mother had known something was up. After Mina got home, Mama had walked over and knocked until Mina finally opened the door. Mama had steered Mina to a kitchen chair and set about making tea as she asked several pointed questions about Barrett Sawyer.

Why was he in town? Was it true he had driven Mina to her appointment in Drogheda? And that they'd had dinner together?

Mama didn't know the identity of the baby's father, but she wasn't stupid. Mina had zero doubt Mama would know the moment she saw Mina and Barrett together.

She was going to have to tell Mama sooner rather than later. She probably should have told her weeks ago, just like she should have told Barrett about the pregnancy.

But she understood better now what her mother had gone through and why she had withheld her father's identity. Although in Mama's case, she had been trying to protect Mina from the fact that her father hadn't wanted her. Mina's only excuse was that she felt humiliated by her choice to spend the night with her boss.

A sigh escaped. Regardless of the changes Barrett had shown over the last couple of days, and that kiss in the garden, she still couldn't see them being a couple. Both their hurts and goals would always come between them.

She didn't want to leave Glenvarra or reside in London. Barrett still lived and breathed work. Even though he'd apologized and been genuinely moved by hearing their baby's heartbeat and seeing it flex its limbs against her belly, he hadn't said anything to make her think he'd changed his views on relationships or marriage. They had a mutual attraction and a baby on the way. But fundamental differences would always keep them apart.

She glanced at the grandfather clock at the far end of the room. Thank goodness. It was almost time for the walkthrough of the new hawking and fairy trail experience. She'd been living and breathing the Autumn Heritage Banquet all morning. Getting outside in the fresh air and having the chance to clear her mind, would be a much-needed respite.

Her phone rang. Relief coursed through her as she answered. "Thomas! Thank goodness, I've been worried sick."

"Sorry to worry you." He sounded tired but relieved, as if a great weight had been lifted off his shoulders.

"How's your friend?"

"Better now. It was touch-and-go for a bit, but…" His voice trailed off, and he cleared his throat. "I'm sorry I had to run out on you."

"No, Thomas, I understand. Truly. And I'm glad your friend is okay. Anyone I know?"

"No, just a friend from technical school."

Mina frowned. Thomas had gone to the Galway Technical Institute after secondary school. It made sense that he would still have friends in Galway. But something in his tone was off. Was Thomas lying to her?

"Okay. Well… I'm glad they're all right," she finally said.

"Thanks. I should be back on Saturday in time for the gala. And look, Mina, I know I owe you an explanation. And an answer."

Dread pooled in her stomach. That didn't sound like a prelude to a yes. "It's all right." She swallowed past the sudden thickness in her throat. "Focus on your friend, and we'll talk when you get back. Got to run."

She ended the call before Thomas could say anything else. She shoved her phone in her pocket and let her head fall back.

God, what was she going to do if Thomas said no? She'd mentally prepared herself for the task of finding someone else. But the thought of actually marrying someone she worked with, or, worse, barely knew, made her feel drained.

Except there was no alternative. Not if Bridget chose her offer over Barrett's.

You could ask Barrett.

The thought sounded in her mind before she could stop it, but she quickly squashed it. She and Barrett may be trying their hand at a partnership when it came to the baby, but in business, they were rivals. There was no way he would marry her if he knew that was the only way for her to secure her inheritance and finance the renovation.

Besides, even if he did agree to such an arrangement, it would be different. A name-only marriage to Thomas would be a fun secret between friends, one with inside jokes and a nice payday waiting at the end.

Marriage to Barrett, on the other hand, would be a year of temptation, of trying not to hope that they could turn it into something real.

She walked out of the hall and collided with a firm body. A hand settled on the side of her belly.

"Oh, excuse me..."

She looked up, her heart slamming into her ribs at the sight of Barrett. His hand curved, pressing against her stomach with a firmness that felt possessive. Protective. It thrilled her.

He smiled down at her, a genuine smile that made her pulse jump as he removed his hand. She nearly leaned forward, asked him to touch again. What would it be like to have his hand on her stomach, to feel their baby move as she laid her hand on top of his? The intimacy of it nearly stole her breath. "One of the front desk attendants said you were in here," he said. "I just had a tour of the spa."

She mentally steadied herself. "I hope you liked it. Bridget opened it over ten years ago, but she's always evaluating how to make it better."

"Not what I was expecting in a small village on the coast of Ireland. Although," he added with an arched brow, "styling it after a traditional Roman bathhouse was surprising."

Mina wrinkled her nose even as she smiled. "At least I talked Bridget into putting up a sign acknowledging that the Romans never had baths in Ireland the way they did in England. People still enjoy the aesthetic, and that is good business. I keep meaning to book a massage."

"With the whirlwind life you're living, I'd say you need more than one."

"I like staying busy."

He tipped his head to one side. "But no longer because you have to."

Shocked by his perceptiveness and his memory, she looked away. "No," she finally said. "No longer because I have to. I forgot I told you that," she'd murmured.

"That if you slowed down too much, it gave you time to think about what was still missing in your life."

Because she'd been a naive, greedy fool. She'd had so much right here in Glenvarra the whole time.

"Being in London was good for me in many ways. Most importantly, it helped me realize Glenvarra will always be home." She glanced over her shoulder at the banquet hall. "Similar to how focusing on how great of a parent my mom was versus pining for a father who deserted us. Sometimes we don't see the good right in front of us." She turned back to him. "I'd be lying if I said that ache was completely gone. But since I returned from London, I've been more content than I've ever been. Even before my grandmother's will reading and learning that my father had passed, I was more content."

"What changed?" he asked.

Experiencing my own heartbreak. The fallout with Barrett had made her appreciate her mother and the choices she had to make. She'd always enjoyed living in Glenvarra. But coming home to the winding streets she could walk blindfolded and the familiar faces who welcomed her with open arms had made Mina realize just how blessed she'd been all along.

But saying that aloud would reveal just how deeply she had allowed herself to fall for Barrett back in London. Not only did she not want to share that, but she truly didn't want to hurt him or make him uncomfortable.

"I changed," she finally said. She glanced back at the clock again, then frowned. "I'm sorry, I have an appointment."

"When is—" Barrett began, but she held up a hand.

"I know we need to talk things out about the baby. But I need to do this walkthrough for a change to one of our excursions."

"Which one?"

"Falconry lessons, followed by a fairy trail hike."

One corner of his mouth curved up. "Falcons and fairies. An interesting combo."

She winced. After their dinner that ended with

that disastrous kiss, she had done little to sell him on the idea of the renovation. She'd made a promise to Bridget, and she knew Bridget was still deciding between their two offers. Acting honorably sometimes felt like self-sabotage.

"It's a small part of our revenue, only a hundred thousand or so, but it's a big draw, and it performs well on social media. Would you like to come?"

"Yes," he said. "I would."

She guided him out a side door and across the green separating the castle from the mews. "We offer forty-five minute private lessons for one-hundred and fifty pounds, plus packages for weddings and special events starting at a thousand. Small group lessons are offered for twenty a person."

"That seems cheap."

"Bridget wanted to keep the experience available to everyone, much like she wants to do with the renovation of the North Wing. We've also been in talks to expand and offer a falconry amphitheater. We'll make that decision next year after seeing if any of the unique experiences we offer between now and then do well."

"Why do you like it?" Barrett asked as they walked towards a large barnlike structure.

"Me?"

"Yes. You wouldn't be going out for a personal look if you didn't care."

"It's the history of it. I'm very proud of my

roots, and falconry has been a part of Irish life for centuries." She grinned. "And I like the fairy lore, too. Never too old for fairy tales."

"I didn't realize it had been around that long. When did it start?"

She paused just outside the doors, suddenly shy. "Once I get started on a historical tangent, it's hard to get me to shut up."

"I'm aware." His voice, warm and amused, had her ducking her head and tucking her hair behind her ear.

"Sometimes I get a little obsessed. I can turn people off."

Leaves crunched under their feet. A light breeze stirred the folds of her cloak.

"Who put that idea in your head?"

Suddenly feeling foolish for even bringing it up, she shrugged. "More just seeing people's eyes glaze over—"

"Uh-uh." Barrett reached over and grabbed her elbow, bringing her to a stop. "Who, Mina?" he gently pressed her.

She tilted her head back to look at him. "An old boyfriend."

Barrett's fingers tightened on her elbow. "How recently was this?"

A dry chuckle escaped. "Three or four years ago. I didn't date much, and the few times I did, they quickly learned my studies came first."

Barrett's lips tilted up at the corners. "A sentiment I can understand."

"Well, Cormac didn't. The night we broke up I finally agreed to take a break studying for an exam and went out to grab a beer. I was telling him about an old mill that was being adapted into an art gallery, and he told me he didn't really want to hear about my obsession just then."

"Tosser."

A snort of laughter escaped. "Barrett Sawyer, I didn't think you were capable of such language."

His smile spread across his face, slow and devastating. "Only when the occasion warrants it."

His hand came up. Mina's breath caught as his fingers caught one of her curls and gently tucked it behind her ear.

"That's one of the things I admired about you, Mina." His voice deepened, slid across her skin with an intimacy that made her shiver. "I've never known someone as passionate about their work as you."

It was very hard to formulate words when he was this close. When he was saying things that eased some of her worst insecurities and looking at her like he...liked her? Cared for her?

"I thought passion and business don't mix."

He inclined his head. "Maybe I was wrong." He released her and stepped back before she could formulate a response. "So, now that we've established your ex was a git, tell me about falconry."

Falconry. Birds. She needed to focus and not think about the warmth still circulating through her veins or the whiplash to her resolve.

"Falconry was introduced in Ireland around the eighth or ninth century. The Brehon Laws even included protections for falcons."

"The Brehon Laws?" he asked.

"Early Irish laws." Her focus returned in bits, although she was very aware of Barrett walking beside her as they neared the falconry. "They covered everything from land ownership to personal injury." When his eyes widened slightly, she grinned. "Right? Cutting down a tree could get you fined, and women could own property and even claim damages if mistreated by their husbands."

Barrett scowled. "Sad that makes it unique for its time."

"Yes, but still remarkable. The laws themselves were outlawed in the 1600s. But going back to falconry, it thrived for nearly a thousand years. Falcons were primarily trained and used as hunters. Specific birds were even tied to rank." She gestured toward the ruins next to the castle. "The tower of the North Wing was used as a falconry in its early years."

"If I remember right, the practice died off for a bit."

Mina nodded. "It started to decline between the eighteenth and nineteenth centuries for a number of reasons. Partly because firearms were introduced for hunting." She sighed, glancing toward the large wire cages at the end of the structure. "But that's also when the state started offering bounties for dead birds of prey, including falcons. They accused them of being pests and targeting farm animals."

She glanced back at the cliffs. "Small groups survived along the west coast and in the north, along the cliffs. Wildlife protections were eventually introduced, and Irish falconers began to breed and train falcons like their ancestors did. A historic tradition and a way of life nearly lost." She turned back to Barrett. "That's why I like it. Hundreds of years later, and we're still engaging in a tradition our ancestors did. I also like the perseverance of the falcon. All the odds were stacked against them, but they survived."

Barrett stared at her. "It is remarkable."

He wasn't talking about the falcons anymore. No, he was talking about *her*. She swallowed hard at the admiration in his eyes. He'd never shown such emotion in London.

What did it mean? And what was she going to do about it?

CHAPTER FOURTEEN

Barrett

BARRETT WATCHED AS Mina chatted with the falconer, a tall man with thick arms and a wiry beard. He smiled slightly as he overheard her ask about the falconer's children.

He never considered himself a people person. But he did like this about her. Which made her dangerous. She didn't just test his tight leash on his control. When he saw her, so genuine and full of warmth, she unknowingly held up a mirror that was hard for him to look at. To be confronted with the fact that he had held himself back for so long not just because he didn't want to get hurt, but because he didn't want to be like his father. For so long he had equated emotion with wildness, unreliability, selfishness. But he'd withdrawn too much, taken his commitment to logic too far.

Now, though, as he gazed out over the Irish countryside, he realized he was no longer content to live his life like that; empty and soulless. He had started to take a harder look at himself these last few days. Largely, out of his desire to be the best father he could possibly be.

But a growing part of it was Mina.

He shouldn't have touched her just now. But when she'd looked up at him, trying to conceal the pain and doubt left by a careless boy too stupid to see the treasure he had in his hands, he hadn't been able to stop himself. Her hair had felt so soft in his hand as he'd tucked it behind her ear. And the way she had looked at him with such wonder, as if she could hardly believe Barrett genuinely liked her fascination with history, had made him want to pull her into his arms and kiss her.

He'd stepped back. She'd made it clear in the courtyard what her preferences were. A sentiment he had agreed with at the time. A sentiment that was becoming harder and harder to abide by the more time he spent with her.

"Mr. Sawyer!" Mina gestured for him to come over. "This is James, our head falconer."

"Pleased to meet you, sir," James said with a strong handshake.

"Likewise. Miss Callahan's been telling me about your operation. Impressive."

James grinned, his teeth flashing white against the red of his beard. "Thank you. I can trace my family roots back to tending the mews of a fourteenth-century Irish lord in the north. And Miss Bridget and Miss Mina have given me an opportunity to follow in my ancestors' footsteps."

Barrett glanced around. "Do you get much business in the fall?"

"October's decent, but November is when we start to slow down," James said. "We have a group scheduled later today and two tomorrow. More this weekend during the Autumn Heritage Banquet."

"Along with a special demonstration in the courtyard during the gala," Mina added. "We're also offering a discounted group class with a bonfire next week. Cider or hot whiskey, and then a guided fairy trail walk at twilight."

"You said fairy trail earlier, and I didn't think to ask what exactly a fairy trail is."

"There are dirt mounds all over Ireland that are said to be the homes of fairies," she explained. "Some people started decorating them, and the trend caught on. A lot of villages and hotels now offer fairy trails that usually feature some type of decoration or scavenger hunt. We enlisted several artisans to do wood carvings of different Irish folklore tales. It's a great option for people who are wanting to get about outside, and it's an excellent addition for families with children."

Yet another marker in Róisín's favor. From everything Barrett had seen so far this week, Bridget and her crew did an excellent job staying in touch with the market, constantly evaluating and looking at how to make things better.

Of course, now he had to contend with Mina's offer and her lack of a stake in ownership. But it was no longer just about expanding Sawyer Development and diversifying their portfolio. He genuinely liked the castle, the town, and the surrounding countryside. He wanted it to do well, not just from a business standpoint but from a personal one.

James grinned at Mina. "Before you go on your walk, would you like to see Theo?"

"If you have the time."

James pulled a glove out of his back pocket and handed it to her. "Be right back."

As he walked off, Mina started to pull on the glove.

"Is that safe to do while you're pregnant?"

Mina frowned, but when she looked at his face, her expression softened. "The falcons here are well cared for. They're kept in a safe, clean environment, and they have excellent veterinary care." She held up her gloved hand and waggled her fingers. "Plus, as long as I wear the glove, I'm safe."

James walked back out. "He's ready and waiting for you."

Barrett glanced around. "Where?"

Mina held up her arm, her eyes sparkling and her smile radiant. "Watch this."

James placed what looked to be a small piece of food on top of Mina's outstretched hand. There was a rustling of leaves from one of the nearby trees, and then a large falcon swooped down toward them, its wings outstretched. It landed on

Mina's arm, its claws wrapping around the leather as it plucked the food from her hand and scarfed it down.

Mina laughed. "Hello, Theo." She grinned at Barrett. "Amazing, isn't it?"

"It is." And he meant it. The bird was magnificent.

"Do you want to try?"

His first inclination was to say no.

"Come on." Mina held her arm up a fraction, an encouraging smile on her face. "When's the next time you'll have a chance to do this?"

"If my offer wins, perhaps quite a bit."

She narrowed her eyes, and he wouldn't have put it past her to stick out her tongue at him if James hadn't been watching. "Take a moment for yourself, Barrett."

It was using his name that did it. The first time she'd said his name in casual conversation in front of someone else.

She shouldn't have this kind of power over him. But as he watched her standing there with the falcon resting on her arm and the sun playing in her hair, he experienced a sense of déjà vu. Just like the moment he'd been introduced to the new spring intern and she'd held out her hand with a smile radiating pure excitement. Her projects weren't merely checklist items on the way to some bigger goal. She threw herself into everything with a passion he had once avoided. Despite her own pains and losses, she exuded life.

And she made him want to try living again. Not just existing, not just marching on to the next acquisition, but truly living.

"All right."

James walked over and held out another glove. "Once you've got the glove on, hold up your arm steady. I'm going to call the falcon over. Ready?"

James let out a sharp whistle. The falcon took off from Mina's arm and soared over to Barrett. He held his ground as the falcon's claws wrapped around his arm and folded its wings into its sides before turning its head to look directly at him.

A primal thrill rushed through him, more potent than any acquisition or boardroom achievement to date. Here there was nothing but sky and woods and the incredible creature perched on his arm.

"I can see why this is so popular," he finally said.

James reached over with his own gloved hand. Another soft whistle, and the falcon hopped off Barrett's arm onto James's glove.

"Thank you."

"You're welcome." James grinned. "Come back anytime."

Mina walked up to him as he took off the glove. "Well?"

"Definitely never something I thought I would do."

"Did you like it?"

"I did." He gave her a small smile. "Thanks for sharing this with me."

Her own smile disappeared as she looked up at him with something akin to confusion. He understood. Every moment he spent with Mina deepened his own confusion about what exactly he was going to do at the end of the week. The thought of going back to London, of leaving her and the baby here, tied his stomach into knots.

But what would extending his time here say about his feelings and intentions toward Mina? After both his and her repeated insistence that they weren't right for each other, would she even be open to considering something more?

"Hey, Mina!"

James's call broke through.

Mina blinked and stepped back from Barrett. "Yes?"

"Since you're down here, do you mind checking out the brochures Orla had printed? My wife," James clarified to Barrett. "She started up her own printing business in town last spring."

"And is now the exclusive printer for Róisín by the Cliffs," Mina added.

James's proud smile made Barrett blink. His parents had never once looked like that. They'd never been proud of each other, happy for the other's success.

"Do you want to come in?" Mina asked as she started to follow James into the barn.

"I'll stay out here." Barrett nodded toward the cliffs. "Not a view I'll get to see every day."

Mina's smile slipped. She nodded and disappeared into the barn.

Barrett faced Róisín and slid his hands into his pockets. The sun sank behind him, casting rays that painted the limestone walls of the castle a rich, golden color. Even the North Wing, with its jagged towers and crumbling facade, looked magical.

He shook his head. He was starting to think like Mina.

His phone vibrated in his jacket pocket. He pulled it out and glanced at the screen, then frowned.

"Bridget? Is everything all right?"

"Hi, Barrett." The slight waver in Bridget's voice told Barrett this wasn't going to be a good call.

"What's wrong?"

"The structural engineer who evaluated the castle came out to evaluate the crack you and Mina saw. He said he went back and did some additional digging in the archives." Her breath came out on a shuddering gasp. "Apparently a load-bearing wall was removed fifty years before the fire."

Barrett's eyes closed. "I'm sorry, Bridget."

"He's coming back out to confirm, but I don't… He's the best."

"So, what does that mean?"

"Twenty million for a rebuild if we keep the original design and follow all heritage guidelines." Bridget paused. "I understand this changes the scope of the project significantly, and the engineer and his architecture team said they can readjust for smaller rooms, fewer floors—"

"Let's wait and see. But I'm willing to increase my financing to twenty million."

For a moment, Bridget said nothing. Then, as if she couldn't quite believe what he'd just said, she murmured, "You are?"

"Yes. You have a business worth investing in."

"I can't thank you enough. I still need to run numbers and make sure we're solvent with the additional financing required." She hesitated. "Could we keep this between us for now? Mina told me she informed you she was behind the other offer. I doubt she'll be able to increase her offer, but I don't want her to know until we know for sure. Especially with the baby and the banquet coming up."

Barrett's fingers tightened on the phone. This was going to hurt Mina in more ways than one. He wanted to tell her now. But he understood Bridget's reasoning, and ultimately it was her choice to make. "Yes, I agree. I'll submit a new proposal and update the amount to twenty million so you have it in writing."

Barrett hung up and stared at the North Wing.

The sun had sunk down behind the main castle. Now the ruins looked dark, like twisted fingers stretching out of the ground trying to escape the dirt.

Definitely too much time in make-believe land.

He honestly believed in the hotel's ability to make good on his investment. It was a unique and prosperous business, and he wanted to support its development. But this was the part he hated about working with old buildings; the unfortunate surprises, the numerous factors outside his control.

"Everything okay?"

Barrett turned and inwardly swore as Mina approached. How much had she heard?

Not much, he decided, judging by her relaxed smile. Bridget wanted to be the one to tell Mina herself. And he, selfish bastard that he was, didn't want to ruin the camaraderie that had developed between them over the last two days.

"Just a quick chat with a client."

"I was hoping to walk the trail, but I just got a text that I'm needed back at the castle."

"Go on without me. I'm going to walk the trail a bit."

She nodded and started to turn away, but he caught her hand in his. She stopped and slowly looked up at him with a shy smile that kicked his pulse into high gear.

"Thank you, Mina. For yesterday and for this."

Before she could respond, he gave in to impulse and leaned down to press a gentle kiss on her cheek. It would be so easy to turn his head, to capture her mouth with his.

Slow. Steady.

"You're welcome, Barrett."

His body tightened. Surely at some point he would get tired of hearing her say his name like that. Yet as she pulled the hood of her cloak up and turned toward the castle, he couldn't imagine going another seven months without hearing her voice.

Which left him with one hell of a problem.

He watched her walk back until she was no more than a small figure disappearing into the side entrance.

He started off down the fairy trail, marked by two solar lanterns glowing warmly as the sun continued to sink farther behind the castle. Beech and hawthorn trees lined the path, branches twining overhead and offering speckled shade as an afternoon chill set in. Every dozen feet or so was a wooden sculpture of a fairy, mermaid, or some other mystical creature. Whimsical, enchanting.

He barely paid attention to the artistry. He couldn't when all he could see was that look of trust on Mina's face.

Logically he knew he was doing the right thing. He was honoring Bridget's request. But he knew that when Mina learned the truth, she would be heartbroken. Sawyer Development being selected would sting.

But it would be the demolition of the North Wing that would hurt the most.

He stopped in the middle of the trail. This was no longer just about Róisín or the baby. This was about Mina and his growing feelings for her.

So, what the hell was he going to do about it?

His initial plan had included finalizing his offer with Bridget the Monday after the gala. He had a flight to London booked for Monday afternoon and a tentative schedule for meetings and site visits for the renovation. A renovation that would now include a demolition.

And then what? Was he going to be able to live and work over five hundred kilometers away? Only see his child on weekends and school holidays? Only see Mina in passing?

But what other choice did he have? Mina had made it clear she didn't think they were a good fit. And not without reason. He had confused himself with his inconsistent words and actions, with how quickly his emotions had evolved. Was he capable of offering what she deserved? Of truly letting down his walls and letting her in?

A question he didn't have an answer to. And that answer would have to be a definitive yes if he were to ask Mina to consider anything beyond the coparenting relationship they'd agreed upon.

It would hurt. It would hurt like hell to give up on pursuing more. But it was the right thing to do.

A carved fairy caught his eye. The artist had arranged her so that she was peeking out from behind a tree. Wooden hair spilled over her shoulder and partially covered one elegant wing. Her lips were carved into a teasing smile, as if she knew the lies Barrett was telling himself.

CHAPTER FIFTEEN

Mina

BUTTERFLIES FLUTTERED IN Mina's stomach as she glanced at the ballroom door. She'd been on pins and needles all morning. Yesterday's unexpected outing with Barrett had left her reeling. It should have been a simple business excursion, a chance to show off Róisín.

But business excursions didn't include having her hair tucked behind her ear or being kissed on the cheek.

"Good morning, Mina."

Mina looked up, then frowned as Bridget walked closer. There were deep circles beneath her eyes, and her skin was paler than normal.

"Are you all right?"

Bridget waved a hand. "Just a lot on my mind."

Guilt trickled in. "The renovations?"

"The renovations, the gala, plans for the winter." Bridget shrugged, but it didn't mask the worry. "Perhaps I should have waited until after the gala before having Mr. Sawyer out."

Mina's stomach rolled. Not the baby, just good old-fashioned guilt. Why had she made her pitch to Bridget without securing Thomas's yes first? Because she'd panicked. Now she was all but certain Thomas was going to say no, leaving her fiancé-less and without the bulk of her inheritance unless she found another groom. Marrying Thomas had been unappealing at best before Barrett had reentered her life. Now the possibility of it almost felt betrayal.

Just like she'd be betraying Bridget if she didn't tell her the truth. It scared her. But it was the right thing to do.

"Bridget, there's something I need to tell you."

"Mina, if it's about the proposal—"

"I didn't tell you everything about my inheritance." Mina blew out a harsh breath. "In order to get the full amount, I have to get married within a year."

Bridget's mouth dropped open. "Seriously?" At Mina's nod, Bridget shook her head. "That's absurd."

"Pretty much what I said. Look, I should have told you, but I thought I…well, I thought that was going to be taken care of."

"You weren't planning on marrying someone just to finance the renovation, were you?"

"No! No, I want that inheritance for the baby and me. When I made the offer, I thought I had an arrangement that would ensure I'd get the money.

But I don't think my original plan is going to work."

"Meaning your offer no longer stands?"

"It does. I'm going to have to get married to claim my inheritance regardless." Mina looked down at her clipboard. "I just… I wanted to be honest. I should have told you from the beginning. It wasn't fair of me to make that offer before I was married and the inheritance was guaranteed."

Would Bridget be hurt? Angry? Surely she wouldn't be so upset that she would fire Mina, although Mina wouldn't completely blame her if she did. She'd left out an incredibly important detail on her offer, one that could have significant repercussions for Bridget and the castle's future.

Bridget laid a hand over Mina's. "Mina, it's all right."

Mina swallowed hard. "It's not, though."

"Look at me, Mina." Mina slowly raised her head to see Bridget smiling at her. "I meant what I said. Your baby is so fortunate to have you as a mother. Yes, the clause on your inheritance would have been nice to know about. But I know you wouldn't have made the offer in bad faith."

"No." Mina shook her head. "No, I truly thought… I thought I had it all planned."

"You usually do." Bridget leaned in and wrapped an arm around Mina's shoulders. "But sometimes it's okay if things don't go according to plan."

"I know."

"You know that here." Bridget gently tapped Mina on the forehead. "But when it comes to your heart, you hold yourself back."

Before Mina could reply, Bridget gave her a quick hug and then stepped back. "We'll talk on Monday. Go through all our options. For now, though, I want you to focus on the gala and making it a success." She hesitated, as if she wanted to say something more, but then she shook her head. "Monday. We'll talk Monday."

"All right. And, Bridget? I'm sorry."

Bridget gave her another small smile. "I forgive you. I hope you'll forgive yourself, too." She left the ballroom, her steps hurried.

Mina wanted to go after her, see if there was anything she could do to ease whatever burden Bridget was carrying. But she had a job to do. The best way she could help Bridget was by making sure the Autumn Heritage Banquet was a success.

As the morning wore on, Mina should have started to feel tired. She crisscrossed the ballroom at least a dozen times, ensuring artifacts and decor were placed correctly, answering questions from staff.

Instead, she felt buoyed. She had told Bridget the truth and been accepted in spite of her mistakes. She was coming to realize just how much she held trust close to her chest, how few people she'd truly let in to her life. Even those she loved, like her mother, from whom she had also hidden parts of her life.

How long had she had this fear of rejection? Of being abandoned by others like she and her mother had been abandoned by her father?

She looked down at her clipboard and the stack of envelopes tucked beneath the sheaf of papers. What if that was the true reason behind her not telling Barrett about the baby? Had she been so afraid of another rejection that she'd opted for the safer route?

She'd read through the letters she'd written to him last night. As she reread each summary—her first appointment, feeling the baby move for the first time—she'd tasted true regret for not mailing the letters. There was so much Barrett had missed out on, so many milestones he hadn't even known were occurring because she'd chosen fear and pain over doing the right thing.

Which left her with the question of what to do about Barrett and the marriage clause. Just a few days ago, she'd considered it none of his business. But so much had changed in such a short time. She needed to think it through first, not jump straight into it like she had in making her offer to Bridget.

"Mina?"

She looked up and smiled at the head chef. "Sorry. My mind's going in a thousand different directions."

"Understandable," the chef said with a grin as

he held out a silver tray. "Tasting tray for your approval." Delicious smells wafted up: rich butter, freshly baked bread, chopped herbs. "You should sit. Take a break."

Mina nodded and followed him to one of the tables. "That sounds like a great idea."

She glanced over just in time to see Cade, one of the hotel's handymen, and Barrett walking in carrying a large, heavy box. Her pulse stuttered as Barrett grinned at something Cade said. He seemed so happy, relaxed.

"I'll be back in a second," Mina said to the chef. She walked toward the men as they were setting the box against the wall.

"Hello, Mina," Cade greeted her with a smile.

"Hello." She nodded to Barrett, trying to contain the renewed fluttering in her chest. "Good morning."

"Good morning." His gaze was warm and appreciative as he motioned toward the box. "An item for the auction. Just came up from town."

Cade turned and shook Barrett's hand. "Thanks for helping."

"You're welcome."

"You and Cade seem friendly," Mina said as Cade walked away.

"Met him outside when he was unloading the box. Definitely a hard worker."

"That was always something I liked about you. You knew every employee's name, how long they'd been there… It impressed me that a CEO of your stature would bother to learn."

Barrett stared at her for a moment before glancing around the banquet hall. "I realized, watching you interact with my staff, that you genuinely wanted to talk to them. I told myself I was investing in my employees, but really it was just another checklist item. I memorized facts, but there wasn't genuine concern or interest." His back stiffened. "I did it because I was trying not to be my father, not because I genuinely wanted to."

Touched by his honesty, Mina paused, gathering her thoughts. "Well," she finally said, "it's still something I like about you. Are you busy?"

He stepped closer. "I have a meeting in twenty minutes, but I doubt they'd start without me."

Mina laughed. "I need to write that down. The first time Barrett Sawyer ever offered to push back a meeting."

Barrett glanced around the ballroom. "It's been nice being here, not having my schedule packed every minute of the day."

Yes, Mina thought, Ireland suited him. But was it the kind of place a man like Barrett could settle in and be happy? Or was it just the novelty of being away from London? "Do you like seafood?"

His smile grew slightly. "Yes."

"The chef just brought out samples for tomorrow night's dinner. I can taste some of them, but a few are off-limits in my condition."

"Sure." He followed her to the table and pulled out her chair.

"We have smoked salmon on brown bread with seaweed butter," she said, "and an oyster trio—baked with lemon, poached with wild garlic cream, and raw with beer foam. There are mini boxty blinis with dill crème fraîche, goat cheese tartlets drizzled with heather honey, and this—" she picked up a tiny glass "—potato and leek shooters."

"I'm guessing you had a hand in all of this," Barrett said, picking up a tartlet.

"Not the cooking. I do okay with baking, but I haven't explored much else."

He bit into the tartlet. "Tastes incredible."

"The heather honey is actually made from native flora. It's been prized for generations for its flavor and its healing properties."

Barrett smiled at her. "You know, the depth of your knowledge is truly remarkable."

"Thank you." Her cheeks warmed. "I spent hours reading as a kid. First my mom and grandmother read to me, and then once I learned to read, I don't think I ever stopped."

"What books did you like as a child?"

"Anything. Mystery, adventure, fantasy. I read *The Flight of the Doves* and *The Singing Cave* until the pages were worn and the spine was cracked. But I also really loved *Anne of Green Gables*. What about you?"

Barrett spread seaweed butter on a piece of bread and added smoked salmon. "My parents never read to me."

Was it any wonder, Mina thought, savoring the warm, rich soup, that Barrett struggled to share? She had been so fortunate to have a loving parent. Barrett had grown up alone, isolated.

"Perhaps, before you leave," she said softly, "we could pick out a book for you to read to the baby when it arrives."

Barrett stilled. Then, slowly, he nodded. "I'd like that. Are you here for the rest of the afternoon?"

"I actually need to run into town for a dress." She wrinkled her nose. "The one I planned to wear no longer fits. Apparently, this baby decided to grow more than expected."

"Where are you going?"

"There are a couple of boutiques in town. There won't be much, but anything that fits will have to do," she laughed.

"What about Dublin?"

"Dublin's over an hour away, and my car is still in the shop. Besides, I don't think I can justify being away from Róisín two nights before the gala."

Barrett nodded. "Fair. What's left to do?"

"Well..." Mina consulted the checklist on her clipboard, conscious of the letters just beneath. "Review lighting for the ballroom, courtyard, and library. Make sure signage is in place. Reconfirm arrival times for the musicians and our VIP guests."

"Which will take the rest of the night?"

"Well, no, but—"

"You know what I see when I look around the ballroom? A well-organized event that's been double- and triple-checked. Employees who are following out every instruction to the letter." He leaned in. "And an events coordinator who has been working nonstop to plan not only this gala but keep her regularly scheduled events on track, too. All while growing a child."

"Um…well, while that may be true, I still—"

"You've been shouldering this pregnancy alone for the last seven months."

"Five," she muttered. "I didn't know the first two months."

"Semantics aside, you've been doing it alone. I'd like to do something for you, even if it's just a car ride and taking you to a store."

"I don't want you to think you have to buy your way into the baby's life," she finally said quietly.

"I don't. I just want to do something nice for the mother of my child. If you say no, I'll go back to my room and see you tomorrow or at the gala on Saturday. And," he added quietly, "whatever you wear, you'll be beautiful."

It was only by threading her fingers together and squeezing them as tightly as she could that

Mina prevented herself from reaching over to lay her hand on top of Barrett's. There were too many staff milling about.

Finally, she looked up at him. "I'd like to spend some time with you."

CHAPTER SIXTEEN

Barrett

EVEN IN THE darkening hours of an autumn evening, Dublin thrived. People crowded the sidewalks, pouring in and out of shops, pubs, and restaurants. Red-brick buildings lined the streets, interrupted here and there with glass-fronted stores and sleek hotels.

Very different than the cozy, winding streets of Glenvarra. It was interesting, Barrett thought as he navigated through the traffic. He thought he would miss the city more. But while it was pleasant being back in a metro area, there was no sense of coming home, of being back where he belonged.

He glanced over at Mina. She stared out the window, soaking in every detail she could. Quiet satisfaction settled in his chest at getting to do something for her and just her. To enjoy time with her without having to be aware of who might be watching or listening.

His eyes dropped down to her stomach. It was becoming harder to picture leaving her here in

Ireland. It was also becoming harder to picture going back to London.

He'd never imagined himself living outside of the city. The longer he spent in Glenvarra, the more he realized the tension he had unknowingly carried for so many years was dissipating. He was happier, more content. Yes, he still fielded numerous phone calls, video conferences, and emails throughout the day. He was still making decisions and checking in on numerous projects across England and Scotland.

But unlike London, where he always felt on edge, anticipating the next event, here he took a few moments to slow down. Savored a cup of coffee in the morning or to step outside and watch the waves of the ocean rise and fall.

And, above all, enjoyed his time with Mina. Sometime in the last day or so he had finally accepted he was spending time with her not just for the baby or to learn more about Róisín. No, he was spending time with Mina because he wanted to.

But when she learned that Bridget had selected Sawyer Development over Mina's offer...would Mina still look at him the way she had yesterday at the falconry? When she discovered that Barrett had known for days and not told her?

Ironic, he thought sourly as he drove into a car park. He had accused Mina of hiding things from him, cut her out of his life for it. Now the roles had flipped.

As he opened Mina's door, he savored the feel of her hand in his. Savored her smile as he helped her out of the car. And tasted fear for the first time in years. Fear that he may have finally found something worth opening himself up to only to lose it.

The boutique on Grafton Street took up the first two levels of a red-brick structure sandwiched between a historic-looking building and a more modern one constructed out of steel and glass. Mina's preferred style versus his.

Mina's eyes widened as Barrett escorted her in.

"I can't afford this place," she hissed as she took in the crystal chandeliers and tufted antique chairs arranged throughout the store. Mannequins on daises were dressed in silk, chiffon, and taffeta. Long mirrors trimmed in copper were placed every few feet.

And in the middle were rows upon rows of dresses. The kind of dresses he imagined a dreamer like Mina had envisioned wearing herself. The kind of dresses her mother hadn't been able to afford.

"You can afford them now," he murmured, surprised when Mina flinched. "What's wrong?"

"It's just…" She bowed her head. "I don't want to be like my father. It's why I haven't bought a new car yet. I don't want to blow through my money before I even have it."

He hadn't thought it possible to respect her even more. But he did. "You're not like him, Mina. Or my parents."

Mina chuckled. "That might be the kindest thing you've ever said to me."

"I mean it, Mina." He waited until she looked up at him, until he knew she was hearing his every word. "I never saw myself having kids. But I'm very glad you're the mother of our child."

Mina stared up at him. "Barrett..."

"I'm on my way!" The sound of heels clicking on the hardwood broke the spell between them.

"If you don't find something here, we'll go somewhere else," Barrett replied as an attendant came forward to greet them.

"Welcome to the Copper Atelier of Dublin." The attendant, a round-faced woman with long, sleek silver hair, gave them a big smile. "My name's Sarah. How can I help you?"

"I need a dress for a gala tomorrow night. One that fits this." Mina gestured to her belly.

"Of course. We have numerous empire-waist gowns that would look lovely on you," the attendant assured her.

"I am trying to stay within a budget."

"We have a wide range of prices. I'm confident we can find something that you'll both like and be comfortable with purchasing."

Looking relieved, Mina thanked her and wandered toward a mannequin wearing a long, red gown.

Sarah waited until she was sure Mina wasn't looking before she glanced at Barrett. He shook his head, eliciting a knowing smile from the attendant.

Sarah walked Mina up and down the rows. It was fun seeing Mina like this, outside of a professional environment. Watching her eyes light up over one dress, wrinkling her nose in distaste at another. Sarah caught on quickly to what Mina liked and didn't like, and within a few minutes had amassed half a dozen dresses for Mina to try on.

"Why don't you try that last style?" Sarah called over her shoulder. "See if there's anything else you want to add, and then we'll start trying dresses on. Your husband mentioned that you're on a tight schedule?"

Mina blushed, then glanced at Barrett. "Um, yes, we are."

"Perfect. Then I'll make sure to keep things moving." She disappeared to the back.

Mina waited a moment before she whirled around to face Barrett. "What did you say to her?"

"I asked if she had dresses that would fit a woman who was seven months pregnant and, if so, could we please come out tonight and look. That's all."

Mina stared at him for a long moment before shaking her head and turning away.

It was interesting, Barrett thought, as Mina wandered down the last row. He had never imagined himself as a husband, just as he had never thought of himself as a father.

But now, as he watched her run her fingers over a violet-hued dress, he let himself imagine it. Coming home to her and their child. Stopping by the castle to visit her and bringing their son or daughter to explore the nooks and crannies. There was no sense of a trap closing around him, as he had when past girlfriends had pressured him to break his rule and consider a commitment.

No, when he envisioned such a life with Mina, he felt much the way he did these past few days in Ireland. Happy. Content.

Mina's soft gasp caught his attention.

"What is it?"

"Just this dress." She smiled. "It's beautiful."

"Why not try it on?"

"It's outside my budget. Besides, the attendant found plenty of other beautiful dresses for me to try on." She looked back at him and gave him a small smile. "Thank you again."

He waited until she disappeared toward the dressing rooms before he got up and walked over to the last row. He saw the dress and knew instantly which one had caught Mina's eye: a gown the same ethereal blue as sea glass. The skirt of the dress fell in soft folds from the bodice. Silk tulle, so delicate it was almost translucent, extended from the bodice to the neckline and was decorated with silver and crystals in the shapes of flowers. The sleeves were long and loose.

Like fairy wings.

He glanced at the price tag and couldn't help but chuckle. Unlike the other women he had dated, Mina didn't go for flashy or the most expensive. The dress was stunning but elegant. Yes, it was almost two thousand euros, but he'd had women send him bills for dresses, purses, and jewelry five times that.

He'd never once cared what his money was buying. But now, as he walked back toward the dressing rooms, he found himself caring very much.

The dressing room area was just as elegant as the showroom. A wall of mirrors took up the far end. Gold doors lined either side of the room, with royal blue curtains adding a touch of old-world elegance.

Sarah stood near the front of the dressing room, sorting through several dresses hanging from a rack. She glanced over her shoulder, smiling when she saw the dress Barrett carried. "Oh! That just came in last week. It would look beautiful on her. Would you like me to take it in to her?"

"Actually," Barrett replied softly, "I was hoping to surprise her with it when she came out."

Sarah gave him a conspiratorial smile. "I'll just step up front and see if any other clients have come in."

A moment later, the door to Mina's dressing room opened.

"I don't think that last one—oh!" Mina crossed her arms over her chest, one hand clutching at the lapels of a silk dressing gown. "What are you doing back here? Where's Sarah?"

"She went up front to see if anyone else has come in." He held up the dress.

Mina looked longingly at the gown before she shook her head. "Barrett, I only have twenty-five thousand euros from my inheritance so far, and if Bridget were to go with my offer, I need to keep as much of the fifteen million available—"

He ignored the rush of guilt and held the dress up higher. "Try it on, or I'll start knocking percentages off my offer."

Mina huffed. But she couldn't conceal the want in her eyes as she reached out and ran a finger over the silk. "Fine."

She took the dress and disappeared into the dressing room. Barrett settled down in a plush chair arranged in front of one of the mirrors.

"Are you still out there?" Mina's muffled voice sounded through the door.

"I am."

Mina sighed. "It's beautiful."

"So come out and let me see it."

The door opened. Mina stepped out.

His thoughts scattered in a thousand different directions as she walked with light steps toward him, her eyes shy and her smile sweet. His fingers tightened on the arms of the chair so he didn't reach for her.

She was stunning. Gorgeous. The bodice of the

dress clung in all the right places. The flowing sleeves gave her an ethereal appearance.

Fairy wings.

Her hair spilled over her shoulders in red-gold curls. The transparent material just above the bodice gave the illusion that the crystal and silver flowers were resting on her skin. He wanted to press his lips to her cheek, then trail them down to the hollow at her throat before…

It took considerable effort to pull himself back. But… "You look beautiful."

Mina walked over to the mirrors, her skirts rustling. She turned this way and that, her hand settling on the swell of her stomach. "It's very tempting."

"Let me buy it for you."

Mina spun around. "Barrett, I can't—"

"Why not?" he asked as he stood and walked toward her.

She swallowed hard. "It's just such a personal gift."

"It is."

Mina ran a hand through her hair. "Barrett, I don't know what this is between us. One minute we're kissing in a garden, the next we're arguing. We've both agreed that we're not a good fit—"

"And what if I'm questioning that?"

Mina's eyes widened. "What?"

"I like you. A lot."

Something flickered in her eyes, but it came and went too quickly for him to discern.

"I enjoy your company. I value your opinion and your insight. And we're going to have a child together."

Mina exhaled slowly. "So, what does that mean for us?"

"I'm not sure yet. You have the Autumn Heritage Banquet in two days. But after that, we need to have a long conversation not just about the baby, but about us. For right now, you look stunning in that dress, and I'd really like to buy it for you." He paused, then reached out and grabbed one of her hands in his. Savored the sharp intake of her breath as he brought it up to his lips and brushed his mouth over her fingers. "I've given hundreds of gifts over the years."

Her hand tensed in his. "I'm sure."

A perverse part of him enjoyed the thread of jealousy in her voice. But he kept it buried. Just hearing her talk about her ex-boyfriend yesterday had had him gritting his teeth.

"I've never wanted to buy a gift for someone more than I want to buy this dress for you tonight." He slid his fingers down to her wrist, turned her hand gently until her palm was facing him. She watched him, eyes wide and blue, as he leaned forward and kissed the center of her palm. "Please, Mina."

"Are you…" She cleared her throat even as her

hand trembled in his grasp. "Are you trying to seduce me into accepting a gift from you?"

"I don't know." He kissed one fingertip, then another. Mentally catalogued the way her lips parted, the unevenness of her breath, the curls falling in a silken curtain he wanted to sink his hands into. "Is it working?"

"I was going to say yes after you told me I looked stunning."

"Since I'm on a roll, then, have dinner with me."

"Dinner?" The word came out on a breathless whisper.

"Yes. Our first dinner was about business. I want this one to be just you and me."

"Barrett..."

His heart stuttered as she spoke his name almost the exact same way she had that night in his office. Soft and lilting with a thread of smoky longing that had him wishing they were back at the castle.

But he didn't just want Mina's body. He wanted her, all of her. The moment she'd turned to him in the car and invited him into the appointment, opening herself up to rejection even though he'd just hurt her, his remaining resolve had started unraveling. That and hearing the gallop of their child's heartbeat.

"Say yes, Mina. Just one more yes."

"Yes," she whispered.

He smiled against her hand, kissed it once more,

and then gently released her. He wanted more—so much more—but he needed to move slowly.

The attraction between them blazed as strong as ever. But this wasn't just about one night or satisfying a simple physical need. He had never once considered having a relationship that lasted more than a few months. This was going to take time, investment, and strategy.

Just acknowledging that he wanted more with Mina was a concession. He was deliberately making himself vulnerable, something that went against every fiber of his being.

Yet as she disappeared back inside the dressing room, he couldn't think of any other choice.

CHAPTER SEVENTEEN

Mina

IVY CLIMBED OVER the brick facade of The Hearth on Merrion Square. Gardeners kept the vines from crossing over the paned windows. Pale columns framed the dark blue door. Aside from the gold placard to the right of the door, there were no other indicators that this building housed one of the most luxurious restaurants in Dublin.

Mina glanced down at her plain red dress and checkered coat. "Is this dressy enough?" she asked as Barrett tugged her up the stairs.

He stopped near the top step and turned to face her. He reached up and smoothed the back of his hand over her cheek. She turned into his touch before she could stop herself.

"You look beautiful."

The same compliment he'd uttered not thirty minutes ago. But it had the exact same effect as it had in the dressing room of Copper Atelier. Her heart did a long, slow roll as the butterflies she'd felt that morning fluttered once more in her chest. It left her delightfully dizzy and a touch unsettled.

What had happened in the last twenty-four hours to elicit this change? She wanted so much to embrace it, to think that there could truly be something more between her and Barrett.

That didn't stop fear from whispering in her ear as he opened the door and led her inside.

And she instantly fell in love. The building had once been a town house, probably erected in the mid-1700s. Whoever had renovated it had kept the hall intact, from the polished black-and-white marble floors to the mahogany handrail of the grand staircase.

A maître d' looked up from a black wooden podium that matched the color of both his tuxedo and his sophisticated moustache. He smiled at them. "Mr. Sawyer, welcome." He turned and inclined his head to Mina. "And Miss Callahan. Welcome to The Hearth. We're honored to host you tonight. This way, please."

"Have you been here before?" Mina whispered as they followed the host up the stairs.

"No."

"Then how do they know your name?"

"Sawyer Development financed the renovation. They just opened last month."

Shocked into silence, Mina followed Barrett up the remaining stairs. She mentally catalogued the elaborate plaster ceilings, the oil portraits and landscapes on the walls even as her mind whirled.

The rooms on either side of the second-floor hall were open, the round tables filled with people dressed in suits and expensive dresses. A few cast curious glances their way as the maître d' led Barrett and Mina down the hall. But thankfully no one seemed to recognize Barrett or, if they did, they chose to be discreet.

"The Hearth Room," the maître'd announced as he pulled out a brass key and unlocked a door at the far end of the hall.

The door swung open. Mina's breath caught. It was like stepping back in time nearly two hundred years. A Persian rug woven with dark green and muted gold threads covered the middle of the floor, while dark wood gleamed around the perimeter of the room. The ivory-colored walls were offset by bookcases filled with books Mina guessed were also original. A large fireplace dominated one wall. Logs crackled as a fire burned in the grate, creating a warm glow.

In the middle of the room sat a round table covered with a burgundy tablecloth. Two cane-backed chairs sat on either side. Three votive candles flickered around a small bowl of violet dahlias.

The maître d' pulled out a chair. "May I take your coat, Miss Callahan?"

Barrett stepped behind her and slid the coat off her shoulders as she continued to gaze around the room. He handed their coats and her purse to the maître d', who took care of hanging them on a coatrack in the corner.

"This place is stunning," she finally said as she sank into her chair.

"Thank you, ma'am." The maître d' handed her and Barrett menus before grabbing a crystal pitcher off a side cart and filling their water glasses. "Your waitress will be with you shortly."

Mina managed to control herself until the maître d' walked out. "You financed this?"

"I did."

"But…" She glanced around. "The cornices in the hallway, the floors, the windows… They're original."

"They are. The owner was one of the first clients I worked with in London. He had a restaurant in Knightsbridge until he married and moved to Dublin." Barrett nodded toward the ceiling. "There was a lot of work to be done. But he had a solid proposal, and I knew from working with him he would follow through."

Shaken, Mina stared down at her hands for a moment. "I misjudged you," she finally said. "Back in London."

"Yes and no. I have usually preferred modernity over historical preservation. But," Barrett added as Mina looked up at him, "you reminded me of the value that can still be found in a place like this. I signed the contract two months after you left."

It took a moment for the way he was looking at her to register. That same intense focus, but now with an intimate glow that both thrilled and terrified her. "Barrett, I—"

"Good evening." A woman swept into the room, her blond hair twisted into a bun and her slender figure clad in black pants and black vest over a white dress shirt. "My name's Anna, and I'll be taking care of you this evening. May I start you off with drinks or an appetizer?"

Barrett ordered a brandy while Mina quickly opened her menu and scanned the list of appetizers.

"Mina?"

"A glass of nonalcoholic red wine for me, please. The heirloom tomato tartare sounds good…" Her voice trailed off. "Oh, it has cilantro."

"Is there a food allergy?" Anna asked.

"No, he's just not a fan of cilantro." Mina grinned at Barrett. "I remember when you found the cilantro on top of your dan dan noodles. I thought you were going to throw them out the window."

"To be fair," Barrett replied, "it wasn't included in the description on the website."

"Both the truffle-infused mushrooms and goat cheese bonbons are cilantro-free," Anna volunteered.

Mina glanced at Barrett, who nodded. "Perfect."

Anna left, pulling the door behind her until just a small sliver of light remained.

Mina sat back in her chair, gazing around the room, soaking in every detail.

"You remembered."

Her eyes slid back to Barrett. "What?"

"Cilantro."

"How could I forget?" She couldn't help but laugh at the memory of his handsome face screwed up into an expression of complete and utter disgust. "It was like you'd discovered someone had poured poison on your food."

"I'm surprised you remembered that after all these months."

Something in his voice caught her. A suppressed longing, a pain echoing over years, maybe even decades. A boy whose parents hadn't even bothered to read him a bedtime story.

"I also remember that you like your coffee from the Italian shop in the Borough Market. Surprisingly with a whole tablespoon of sugar. When you're stressed, you play classic American rock. And you once wanted to be a Viking."

Barrett stared at her for a long moment. Finally, he spoke. "When did I ever talk about being a Viking?"

"February staff meeting. You and the chief financial officer were arguing over preservation of the exterior of an office building." Her lips quirked. "He said he wanted to not be shelling out thousands on a new building just to make it look old. And you said you once wanted to be a Viking, but we didn't always get what we wanted."

Barrett smiled slightly. "I remember that now." His smile disappeared. "Why did you remember?"

Moment of truth. A chance to pull back, withdraw, keep herself safe. Or a chance to take a leap. "You intrigued me. Even though I didn't always agree with you or like the high-and-mighty act, I respected you. So, I…paid attention." More than she should have. As much as Barrett had infuriated her, she hadn't been able to ignore her attraction or her curiosity.

"I remember the first time you spoke up in a staff meeting." Amusement laced Barrett's voice. "You asked if I had informed the board about the heritage constraints on the warehouse in the Docklands."

Mina wrinkled her nose. "It got so quiet in there I could hear my own heartbeat."

"I liked it."

"You liked me challenging you?"

"Yes. I didn't always like what you had to say, and I didn't always agree with you, but I never had to question where you stood or what ulterior motives you were hiding."

He'd meant it as a compliment. But with the marriage clause still lurking beneath the surface, she felt nothing but remorse. She had hidden things from him and was still carrying a secret.

Yes, it was her life and her choice to make. Barrett wasn't her lover or her boyfriend. She didn't owe him an explanation.

"I like you. A lot."

Guilt tightened its grip on her chest.

The door creaked open, and Anna walked in with their drinks and appetizers. After taking their dinner orders, she exited, leaving them alone once more.

"You told me that night that not knowing your father made you feel like a piece of you was missing."

"I surprised myself when I entrusted you with that." Mina stared into the fire. "I got used to not talking about him for so long."

"Because of your mother?"

"Yes. I used to make up stories about him when I was a child because every time I asked, she'd just say she'd tell me another time. My mother's mother, my *Mamó*, taught me all about our family history. She knew every building in Glenvarra like the back of her hand and tried to teach me all about her ancestors, like it would fill the hole on my father's side of the family." She shook her head. "Even after hearing the conversation between Mama and *Mamó* about my father, I was still angry at times, resentful that my mother wouldn't tell me about him."

"From what you've said about your mother, you have a good relationship now."

"We do." She traced with her finger a wrinkle in the tablecloth. "I told you I overheard my mom talking to my grandmother and that's how I learned my father left her. But there was more to it. It was Father's Day weekend. I went to pick up a book from the library. There were some girls there from school. They asked why I wasn't celebrating with my father, and when I told them it was just my mother and me, they started teasing me. It was like something exploded inside. I ran home, and I yelled at my mother, telling her I didn't understand why she wouldn't just tell me about my father. I left, went to Róisín, read my book. When I calmed down, I went home and my mother was in the kitchen talking to my grandmother. She was crying. I made her cry."

"You didn't make her cry, Mina."

"But I did. I couldn't just be content that I had a loving mother and grandmother. My mother was crying because she didn't know what the right answer was. She hadn't told me about my father because when my mother told him she was pregnant, he told her he didn't care whether it was his or not, that he didn't have plans for a child in his life. She'd been trying to protect me from learning what a selfish bastard he was."

Barrett reached over and covered her hand with his.

"I felt like the worst daughter in the world," she whispered.

"It's normal to want to know."

"It is." She stood and walked over to the coatrack in the corner where the maître d' had hung her coat and purse. She pulled out the envelopes, held together with a string of twine, and walked back to the table. She held out the bundle to him. "This is for you."

"What is it?"

"Ever since the first day I found out about the baby, I've been writing you a letter." She sat back in her chair. "Not every day, but the first ultrasound, the first time I felt the baby move…" Her voice caught. "I'm so sorry I didn't tell you about the baby. I was scared and hurt, and I nearly made the same mistake in shutting you out."

"And my actions caused that."

She shook her head. "You're not solely responsible—"

"We both made choices, Mina." He stood and circled the table, pulled her to her feet and wrapped his arms around her. "We're here now."

"We are."

Shadows played over his face as the fire danced in the hearth. His eyes darkened a moment before he leaned down and kissed her.

She sighed into his kiss, her arms coming up to wrap around his neck. One hand slid into her hair, and he cupped the back of her head as he deepened the kiss. She held on to him, savored the pressure of his lips against hers, the taste of him.

How could she resist this? Could things truly grow between them?

Somehow Mina summoned the willpower to pull back. "Barrett…" She leaned up, pressed her forehead against his. Their harsh breathing filling the space between them. "You said we needed to talk about us."

"I did."

"Does that mean…" She shook her head. "I don't know what to think."

"I don't, either." He slid one finger under her chin and tilted her face up to his. "What I do know is that the thought of leaving you here in Ireland while I return to London hurts."

Hope kindled in her chest. "Really?"

"How does it make you feel? Me going back?"

"I hate it," she whispered. "I thought I never wanted to see you again, but now…the last few days…"

"I feel it, too."

A shudder traced its way down her spine. "I'm scared."

Barrett gently nudged his nose against hers. "Makes two of us. I've never been in a real relationship."

"Could have fooled me," Mina uttered under her breath.

Chuckling, Barrett leaned down and sealed his mouth over hers once more. When he finally let her come up for air, she was clinging to him.

"I've dated around. But there's been no one but you since that night."

She froze. "No one?"

"No." He reached up and cupped her face. "And even before you, there was no one who mattered. No one who made me question my choice to avoid a relationship."

"There's been no one but you, either."

"I'm glad." He traced his thumb over her lips. "Otherwise, I would have had to hunt them down and challenge them to a duel."

"Why?"

"Because the thought of another man touching you—"

"No," she cut in with a laugh. "No, why now? What changed for you?"

He brought his other hand up, framed her face in his hands. "When you looked at me in the car and, despite the fact that I had just pushed you away, invited me to go in to the doctor's appointment with you. I was already doing a poor job trying not to feel anything for you. But when you gave me that gift, a gift I imagine was incredibly hard to offer, it hit me. I didn't just want to be there for the baby. I wanted you, too."

Wanted. He wanted her. Not just for today or one week or the rest of her pregnancy. Barrett Sawyer wanted her.

"I knew when you told me you wanted to hear me talk. When you listened to me talk about falcons and old laws and fairy trails." She slid one hand down to his chest, savored the beat of his heart against her palm. "You've always listened. I didn't trust you after the way we parted in London, but with everything you've shared and everything you've done, I feel…" A huge smile spread across her face. "I feel happy, Barrett."

Instead of smiling back, Barrett's face darkened. "Mina—"

A soft knock sounded on the door a moment before it creaked open.

"Oh!" Anna stood in the doorway with a silver serving tray in hand. "I apologize, I'll come back—"

"No, please stay." Mina stepped back from Barrett as she smiled at Anna, trying to ignore the trepidation whispering across the back of her neck. "It smells delicious."

"You selected two of our most favored dishes. Duck breast with beetroot and black cherry," Anna said as Mina and Barrett took their seats, "and turbot on the bone with browned butter, capers, and lemon."

Anna withdrew a moment later, closing the door behind her. But instead of relaxing, Barrett looked tense.

"Barrett." Mina waited until he met her gaze. "I want you to know that I'm not…expecting anything."

He frowned. "What do you mean?"

"We both know we don't want this to end yet. But what I said before Anna came in, I'm not pressing for a commitment or anything like that."

Barrett started to speak, but she held up her hand.

"We've shared a lot tonight. More than I think either of us planned. Let's just enjoy the next few days, get through the gala, and then we can talk."

That would give her time to get through the gala and figure out how she was going to bring up the subject of the marriage clause. Whether their time lasted weeks or years, he deserved to know.

It was daunting. Scary. But for the first time in a long time, her hope was stronger than her fear.

Finally, Barrett gave her a small smile. "That sounds like a good plan."

They spent the rest of the meal sharing the kind of details one normally shares on a first date: favorite movies, foods, places they wanted to travel. After a shared dessert of baked lemon tart with mascarpone, they walked hand in hand to the car park near Grafton Street.

It wasn't until they were driving home that Mina let herself revisit that moment before Anna had walked in. The moment when she realized that despite the progress she and Barrett had made, they were both still keeping secrets.

CHAPTER EIGHTEEN

Mina

THE BANQUET HALL was packed. Chandeliers blazed overhead, creating an intimate setting despite the three hundred people milling about. Appetizers were being met with rave reviews as people plucked tartlets and soup shooters off the trays carried by waiters dressed in kilts. Judging by the numbers Mina had glimpsed on the silent auction forms, they were going to raise even more than they'd hoped for the local artist consortium.

Best of all, Mina was happy. Happier than she could have possibly imagined a week ago. There was still plenty of uncertainty, but after their excursion to Dublin, she was hopeful. Barrett wanted her. He cared about her. And she was doing her best to focus on the moment.

Yesterday offered her plenty of chances to practice just that. It had been a whirlwind finalizing everything, reviewing checklists, and calling vendors to confirm. But in between calls, Barrett had followed her into the library and given her a searing kiss behind the drapes, one that had left her weak-kneed and with a ridiculous smile on her face she hadn't able to wipe off. More than one person had commented on how calm she was right before the big event.

It hadn't been until she tumbled into bed that fear had raised its head. Fear about what Barrett was keeping from her. Fear about how he would react when he learned about the marriage clause. Would he be angry she hadn't told him? Would he think she only wanted him to get the money?

No. She wasn't going to think like that. Barrett had given her plenty of reasons to trust him. Tomorrow or Monday they would talk. She would tell him about the marriage clause. And then she would tell him that she was going to withdraw her offer to Bridget.

It stung. But after experiencing The Hearth, after learning more about Barrett's business model and why he did what he did, she knew he would take care of Róisín. Trusted him to do so.

Which would leave them free and clear of any of the inheritance stipulations to hasten their relationship. She didn't like turning down a fortune. But she had a good job, a roof over her head, and a partner by her side.

"There's the mastermind behind all this magic!"

Mina turned to see Arlowe, Ivy, and a handsome man standing behind her. "You made it!"

Arlowe solved the problem of whether or not

to hug by reaching out and pulling Mina into her arms. "We did. We were thrilled to get your invitation."

The dark-haired man behind her held out his hand. "I'm Hart. It's nice to meet you."

"And it's wonderful to meet you." Mina smiled. "Congratulations, by the way."

Hart beamed as he slid an arm around Arlowe's shoulders. "Thanks."

"We're still working out wedding details, but it'll be a few months from now. You'll have to fly over. You and the baby," Arlowe added with an excited grin. "How are you feeling?"

"And how did things go with your ex-boss?" Ivy asked. "Because I know a guy who can open an investigation into his finances."

"Fortunately, they'd find my finances are clean."

Arlowe and Ivy's jaws dropped as Barrett walked up, looking incredibly handsome in a tuxedo.

Ivy was the first to recover. She crossed her arms and arched a brow. "That's what they all say."

Barrett chuckled and held out his hand. "Barrett."

"Ivy," Ivy said. "Mina's long-lost cousin."

"And I'm Arlowe," Arlowe said as she held out her hand, although her eyes were still narrowed in suspicion. "Also a long-lost cousin. And this is my fiancé, Hart."

Barrett nodded to all of them. "It's nice to meet you."

"So…" Arlowe prompted.

Mina glanced up at Barrett, who was gazing down at her with warm affection. "We're working through things."

Both Ivy and Arlowe looked like they wanted to ask more questions but thankfully didn't.

"Well, it's nice to see you happy." Arlowe looked around in wide-eyed wonder. "This place is amazing."

"Thank you for coming." Mina smiled. "I can't believe you both made it."

"Hart and I were in France, so it was easy to pop up here."

"And I like flying." Ivy gave Mina a faint smile. "Thanks."

"Do you mind if I steal her away? Just for a moment," Barrett asked.

When Ivy and Arlowe nodded, Barrett grasped Mina's elbow and guided her out into a corridor.

"What's going on?" she asked.

Barrett glanced this way and that before backing her into a small alcove.

"Barrett!" she said with a laugh.

"I had to tell you how beautiful you looked."

"Well, thank you."

"And," he added as he brought his hand up and cupped her cheek, "I wanted to steal a kiss."

Her heartbeat tripled. "That can be arranged."

He leaned down and sealed his lips over hers. She let out a soft moan against his mouth. She would never tire of kissing him, of having these moments of physical connection.

Barrett raised his head. "I haven't been able to stop thinking about kissing you since yesterday. Am I allowed to request a dance?"

Mina hesitated.

"If not," he said quietly, "I understand."

"No." Mina shook her head. "I told my mom last night. It's only a matter of time before other people catch on."

"How did that go?"

"Surprisingly well."

Mama had been concerned and understandably so. But she'd been worried, not disappointed. When Mina had dared to venture her worst fear, Mama had simply wrapped her in a hug and kissed her forehead, the same way she had always comforted Mina. *I just want you to be happy.*

"I'm glad."

"Me, too." She hesitated. "Maybe we could have coffee with her next week. Tea, something casual. Give you a chance to meet."

"I'd like that." He nodded toward the banquet hall. "Are you going back in?"

"Mina?"

Mina whirled around, a smile splitting her face. "Thomas!" She dropped Barrett's hand and hurried forward, wrapping her friend in a hug. "I didn't know you were coming back today."

"I was hoping to make it in time for the gala." His eyes shifted to a point over her shoulder. "Am I interrupting?"

"Oh." She turned back to Barrett, who was watching Thomas with narrowed eyes. "Thomas Mallory, this is Barrett Sawyer."

Barrett held out his hand. "Nice to meet you."

"Likewise," Thomas replied as they shook hands.

"Thomas and I have been friends since primary school. Oh!" she exclaimed. "How's your friend in Galway? Are they doing all right?"

"Yeah, they're better." Thomas shuffled his feet. "Look, I'm sorry to burst in like this, but do you have a moment?"

"Sure." Mina turned to Barrett. "Can I come find you after I talk to Thomas?"

Barrett's gaze flicked between her and Thomas. Then, slowly, he nodded.

On impulse, Mina leaned up and kissed his cheek. "I'll be just a moment."

His eyes softened. "All right."

Warmth filled her. He trusted her. And she trusted him.

Mina dropped onto one of the chaise lounges tucked into an alcove and leaned back against the cushions. "That feels better."

"Are you really supposed to be walking around

this much in your third trimester?" Thomas asked as he sat next to her.

"I just had a checkup with my doctor. Everything's fine, and I'm officially cleared to work all weekend."

Thomas arched a brow. "And apparently you had a special ride to said appointment."

Mina groaned. "One of the few things I didn't miss about living in a small town. Why is everyone talking about who gave me a ride when my car broke down? Barrett was just being nice."

"So it's Barrett now."

Irritated, Mina sat up. "You were the one pushing me to get him involved. What's changed?"

Thomas reached over and grabbed her hand. "Involved, yes. But it seems like you're getting involved, too. I just don't want you to get your heart broken."

"And I appreciate that. I won't promise that I won't, but Barrett and I... So much has happened the last few days, Thomas. It's been...wonderful." She squeezed Thomas's hand. "Which leads me to something very important. I have to withdraw my proposal."

Thomas's shoulders sagged as his head dropped back. "That might be the best news I've heard all day."

"You don't have to be that excited about it."

"No, it's just... I should have told you from the beginning."

"Told me no?"

He shook his head. "Look, while you were in Austria, I went to Galway for a friend's birthday. Just a small get-together. While I was there, I ran into an old girlfriend."

Mina's mouth dropped open. "What?"

"Deidre."

An image popped into Mina's head of a short woman with a short bob of dark brown hair and a boisterous laugh. "I remember her. You brought her here to Róisín for a date one summer."

"That's right. We dated for a year, but when I graduated, she wanted to stay in Galway, and I wanted to come back to Glenvarra. We ended things amicably enough but…"

"But you still remembered her," Mina said softly.

"Never forgot her," Thomas murmured. "When I ran into her at the party, it was like no time had passed. And all of a sudden it seemed silly that we let two hours separate us. We spent all night talking and when I came back to Glenvarra, we kept texting." His lips quirked. "And then you came back from Austria and proposed."

"Thomas, why didn't you tell me?"

"Because I didn't know what to do. It's not like Deidre and I had been dating."

"But she obviously matters." Mina squeezed his hand. "All you had to do was tell me. I would have understood."

"Yeah, so then you'd have to marry some stranger to get your inheritance." Thomas blew out a harsh breath. "What kind of friend would I be if I didn't say yes? Especially when you offered me so much in return."

"An honest one." Realization struck. "Was it Deidre you went to see?"

Thomas nodded. "She was in a car accident."

"Oh God."

"She's all right. A broken leg and a concussion, but it could have been so much worse." His grip tightened on Mina's. "The thing is, seeing her in the hospital like that… I…"

"You couldn't marry me."

Slowly, Thomas shook his head. "No. I couldn't marry you."

She squeezed his hand. "You realize I would have been angrier if you had agreed to marry me while you were in love with someone else."

A hoarse sound escaped his lips, a mix of a laugh and a choke. "I didn't even see it coming."

"We rarely do," she said softly.

"So does that mean you and Barrett will be getting married?"

"Not necessarily."

Thomas frowned.

"I want to take it slowly," she explained. "I'm telling him about the clause after the banquet, but I'm not planning to marry anymore for the inheritance. My grandmother may have had good intentions, but my relationship with Barrett is more important."

"Wow." Thomas smiled. "You're in love with him."

Her first thought was to say no. She'd started to fall in love back in London, yes, but she'd stopped herself before she'd fallen too deep. This week she'd held herself back…

And failed miserably. Because she was in love with Barrett Sawyer. Not just a little, not a lot, but completely in love.

Before she could reply, Thomas's phone rang. He pulled it out of his pocket, a goofy-looking smile crossing his face as he read the name on the screen. "It's Deidre. I'll be right back."

Sure, Mina thought with a smile as he walked off.

A soft murmur caught her ear. Somebody else out in the hallway, perhaps sneaking kisses or having a quiet conversation. But it was the muted crying that followed soon after that caught her attention.

Mina pushed off the wall and walked down the hall, her head swinging left and right as she looked for the source of the crying. She rounded a corner and saw Bridget sitting in one of the high-back chairs, her eyes red and her face pale.

"Bridget!" Mina knelt down beside her. "What's wrong?"

"I'm sorry." Bridget put a hand to her temple. "We can talk about it later."

"Bridget, whatever it is, I'm here for you."

Bridget sucked in a shuddering breath. "I'm sorry. I should have told you sooner, but I was trying to wait until after the banquet." She swiped at her eyes. "But someone just asked about the North Wing renovations, and I couldn't..." She sucked in a shuddering breath. "The crack in the tower wall..."

Mina's heart sank.

"I had the engineer out earlier this week. He did some digging and found out a load-bearing wall was removed in the late 1800s, about fifty years before the fire."

"Oh, Bridget, I'm so sorry."

Bridget reached out and grasped her hand. "The North Wing is unstable. A renovation is out of the question."

Mina's chest tightened, but she fought to stay calm. She would deal with her own emotions later. "I understand."

"A rebuild is still on the table, although the cost has gone up to twenty million."

Dread crept in, slow and cold. That was the amount she'd heard Barrett tell his client outside the falconry. A proposal with the updated amount. "Twenty million," Mina repeated. "Barrett knew?"

Slowly, Bridget nodded. "I called him four days

ago. I didn't want to tell you before the banquet, but I didn't plan on you finding out like this."

"So Barrett has the contract."

The look Bridget gave her was full of sadness and regret. "He does. I knew you couldn't go that high, and I already had reservations about taking so much of your inheritance. I don't know if anyone else would finance us at all."

"I understand." Mina forced herself to hug Bridget before she stood. She needed to get away. "I need to get back to the banquet, but we'll talk tomorrow, okay? I'm glad you have options, Bridget."

Before Bridget could say anything else, Mina hurried away.

Barrett had misled her. He'd stopped short of outright lying, but the way he'd phrased things outside the falconry, he'd deliberately led her to one conclusion while keeping the truth from her.

She had told him about her counteroffer. She'd been prepared to give him everything. Had accepted that he was the best choice to finance the North Wing, been willing to surrender her inheritance to give their relationship a chance to develop with clauses or constraints.

Whereas he had been making a deal behind her back.

She stopped in the middle of the hallway. Clenched her fists as she fought back tears and anger. For two glorious days, thought she had finally done it; let herself trust a man. Perhaps, someday in the distant future, she would be able to trust again.

Right now, though, she needed to keep the broken pieces of her heart together long enough to survive through the evening. Then, after the guests were gone and the candles had been snuffed out, she would confront Barrett and demand answers.

Even if those answers ground the pieces of her heart into dust.

CHAPTER NINETEEN

Barrett

BARRETT WALKED BACK into the banquet hall. Mina truly had done an excellent job. Hopefully, he and Bridget could tell Mina tomorrow about the proposal and the heightened cost for the North Wing. It would hurt her initially, but he would be there.

Reading her letters had been painful but rewarding. There was so much he'd missed out on. But it had meant something that she'd thought of him, had written to him, had made him feel involved even as she'd struggled with her decision about whether or not to tell him about the baby.

They'd get through the banquet tonight. And then tomorrow, they'd talk about the future. He wanted them to be a family.

He didn't want to pressure her for too much too quickly. She'd made it clear during their dinner at The Hearth that she wanted to take things slow.

But now that he'd let down his walls, he didn't want to go slow. He wanted to put a ring on Mina's finger, wanted her as his wife when they brought their son or daughter home. The thought of being able to see Mina every day, to wake up to her face next to his, to share all the firsts that would come with having a child, had him more excited than he'd been in years.

Not just excited. Alive.

He was already contemplating opening up an office in Dublin to resolve the distance issue.

He walked back into the banquet hall. Arlowe and Hart were dancing. Barrett spied Ivy standing at a cocktail table and made his way over.

"I'm curious," he said, "what gives you access to resources like a corporate financial investigator?"

"I'm a negotiation specialist for Maura Corporate. Fortune 500 companies."

"I've heard of your firm. Impressive."

"And I've heard of Sawyer Development. Also, impressive." She paused. "So, you and Mina?"

"Yes, Mina and me," he said with satisfied confidence."

"Before tonight, I'd only met her at the will, but we've texted a decent bit. She's very kind. I'm not usually a family girl, but I've started to rethink that stance." She pinned him with hard eyes. "Which makes Mina important to me. If you hurt her, I'll ruin you."

"Noted." He smiled slightly. "It's nice to know my son or daughter will have such fierce cousins in their corner."

Ivy's face softened. "I am looking forward to meeting the baby." She shook her head. "I can't believe Mina and Arlowe both found a way to meet the will's marriage clause already."

He stilled. A clause? Mina hadn't mentioned anything about a marriage clause. Dread slithered into his stomach, but he concealed it. Barrett nodded toward Arlowe and Hart. "They seem happy."

"They've been in love for years."

"And they'll be getting married in time to satisfy the clause?"

Ivy shrugged. "Given that the clause required us to be married within a year of the will reading, I imagine they won't wait too long."

A roaring started in his ears, so loud it nearly drowned out the music. He nodded at Ivy. "If you'll excuse me, I see someone I need to speak with."

He walked away, trying to stay calm even as anger surged through him. Mina had made her offer to Bridget at the beginning of the week when she was still staunchly opposed to Barrett having any involvement in the child's life. Which meant she had either been planning on marrying someone else, or she had changed tactics and decided to set her sights on him. Knowing Mina, the latter seemed less likely. But it was still plausible. It wouldn't be the first time someone had tried to trap him into marriage.

But it didn't make sense. They'd slept together

long before her grandmother had passed. Mina had only recently learned about the inheritance. If she had been trying to talk Barrett into marriage, she would have sought him out or at least responded to his text when he said he was coming to Glenvarra.

His mind flashed back to the blond man she'd greeted out in the hall. Thomas Mallory. His stomach pitched. Were he and Mina engaged? Already married?

He pushed open a door and walked out into the hall just in time to see Mina walking towards him. His heart clenched, but he shoved his emotions down. "Mina."

Her head snapped up, her eyes flashing angrily. "Barrett."

"I need to talk to you."

"And I need to talk to you. Why didn't you tell me about the revised cost for the North Wing?"

"And why didn't you tell me about the marriage clause for your inheritance?"

Mina stilled. When her eyes dropped down, it felt like a door slamming shut on the future he had just envisioned with her.

She opened her eyes slowly. "If we're going to have this conversation, let's go into the library."

As soon as the door closed, Mina turned to him and folded her hands. "I had planned on telling you after the banquet."

"You did. But you also made your offer to

Bridget when you still wanted nothing to do with me, which means you intended to marry someone else."

"Barrett—"

"Was it Thomas?"

She crossed her hands over her belly. "I did propose to Thomas after my grandmother's will reading, yes. That was before you texted that you were coming to Glenvarra."

"And you didn't happen to think that was relevant? Didn't think that maybe your fiancé might have an issue with you kissing another man and talking about sharing a life together?"

"We were never engaged!" Her eyes glimmered with unshed tears. "It was going to be a name-only marriage, and Thomas wasn't sure about my proposal in the first place. Then you showed up, and I never imagined things would change between us like this. I'd already decided to withdraw my proposal before Thomas came back tonight and told me he was in love with someone else."

"You could have told me sooner."

"Why? So you could think I was trying to trap you into marriage to secure my inheritance? And," she added, her voice dropping to a vicious whisper, "you could have told me about the North Wing. But you decided to do business behind my back after I told you about my offer. I trusted you."

Trusted. Past tense. Just like that, the words she'd offered him two nights ago in Dublin were rendered meaningless. An illusion that had crumbled within a matter of days.

The roaring swelled for one horrible, cacophonous moment.

And then it vanished, along with his hopes and dreams for a future with Mina Callahan. She'd villainized him without even talking to him first. She'd told him two nights ago she trusted him, that he made her happy. It hadn't taken much for that trust to crack. Had barely taken any pressure for her to withdraw.

"Bridget asked me not to say anything about the revisions to the North Wing project. She wanted to tell you after the ball."

"You could have still told me. I wouldn't have said anything to Bridget."

And he almost had. But he'd chosen to honor his word. Whether or not that had been the right choice was irrelevant now.

"I could have. Just as you could have told me about the marriage clause." He stopped. Mentally prepared himself for what needed to be said even as a deep part of him shouted at him to stop.

"I still want to be involved in the baby's life. But us… You were right that first night in the courtyard. I don't know how to do this, Mina. I don't know how to be a good lover or boyfriend or husband. I don't think you'll ever be able to trust me, and I'm not content with living the rest of my life waiting to find out."

Mina flinched, but she didn't refute his words. She didn't say anything at all.

"I'll be in touch in the next week or so. We can discuss coparenting then."

Before he could do something stupid like stay and ask her to talk, to find a way to make things work, he turned and walked away.

The emotions he had spent his whole life avoiding had led him to this moment. But cold, hard facts had saved him from making a mistake that would have led to an even deeper pain later. Mina didn't trust him. And after tonight's revelation, he wasn't sure he could trust her either. He wasn't willing to risk getting hurt again. That said enough about their fledgling relationship and its potential.

Facts, he reminded himself as he walked out the double doors of Róisín and into the cold night air. He needed to focus on the facts of what had happened and believe that, in time, the feelings he'd let in would disappear. His walls would be rebuilt. He would find a way to balance his life in London with being a father.

And he would find a way to let go of Mina Callahan once and for all.

CHAPTER TWENTY

Barrett

BARRETT STARED OUT over the city, standing in the exact same spot he and Mina had stood that night. It had been almost a week since he had walked out of Róisín and flown back to London. Bridget had formally signed the contract. His public relations firm had written an excellent article on the upcoming rebuild. They'd been surprised at his insistence to include references to events like the heritage banquet, the falconry lessons, and afternoon teas in the library. He rarely had an opinion on such things. They might have raised their eyebrows, but they hadn't asked.

Not like Mina would have.

As he stared down at the sea of steel, chrome, and glass, he felt a pang of longing. He missed Glenvarra, Róisín, the countryside.

Despite his best efforts, he missed Mina.

He'd driven to Dublin the night of the banquet. Booked a hotel room overlooking the bay and gotten up just after dawn to catch the ferry to Holyhead. He'd made the drive to London in less than five hours. After a quick shower at his penthouse, he'd gone in to work, throwing himself into reviewing proposals, emails, anything and everything he could get his hands on.

As long as he'd kept busy, he hadn't thought of her. Or rather hadn't allowed himself to think about her.

But when he'd finally trudged in to his penthouse after midnight and opened his suitcase, he'd spied the stack of envelopes carefully packed in the corner. Mina's letters.

He'd resisted reading them that night, his first night back in London. But when he'd woken up the next morning, he hadn't been able to stop himself. He'd read them through at breakfast, then again that night and every night since.

The days were still filled with work. He'd always been a workaholic. But now he lived and breathed work. If he wasn't sleeping, he was answering emails, scouring websites for new properties, probably driving his team nuts with his interference. He hated it, but it was the only thing that kept the pain at bay.

The pain and the ugly feeling that he had made a mistake.

His phone rang. He crossed his office and circled around his desk. "Sawyer."

"It's Bridget." Bridget's soft brogue washed over him.

"Hello, Bridget."

"Hello, Barrett. I wanted to let you know that a date's been set for the demolition. They begin next week."

"That soon?"

"Yes. They're wanting to clear the foundation before the winter weather sets in. That way they can either work through it if it's a mild winter, or as soon as the weather clears, they can get straight to work."

She rattled off a few more dates. Barrett listened with half an ear, still processing that the North Wing that had stood for hundreds of years would be gone in a matter of days.

"How's Mina taking the news?"

"Better than I expected, although we're both grieving. We both thought things were going in a different direction."

Barrett understood that sentiment far too well. He wanted to be there with her when it happened or take her away from it so she wouldn't have to see the building crumble.

"Will she be there next week?"

"She said she wants to be. She's strong, Barrett," Bridget added softly.

"I know." He paused, then let go of any sense of pretense and asked, "How is she? Overall?"

"Sad. I should have trusted her and told her the truth upfront."

"You were trying to spare her pain."

"I know. But I shouldn't have asked you to keep the truth from her," Bridget murmured. "I think she's missing the father of her child, too."

It took a moment for that to hit. "How long have you known?" he finally asked.

"Not until you left. She got very sad, and every time I mentioned your name, she changed the subject."

"I hurt her."

"As did I. And from what little she said, she hurt you, too."

"A lot of pain going around."

"Yes, but that's what happens when people care about each other."

He let out a harsh laugh. "In my experience, causing someone pain doesn't mean you care. It means you're either too selfish or too screwed up to be in a relationship."

"I'd argue it depends on the person."

A beat of silence followed, then lingered. Barrett didn't know what to say. He wanted to find a way to make this work. But damn it, what if he hurt her all over again? What if they hurt each other?

"I'll talk to you soon, Barrett."

"Goodbye, Bridget."

He hung up and looked back out over the city. He'd thought walking away would be the best thing for both of them. But he hadn't given her a choice. He'd been hurt, so he struck out like a wounded animal. He'd pushed her away.

Again.

He shuddered and pulled out one of her letters, the one from her first ultrasound. He unfolded it, his eyes devouring the loopy cursive.

I've toured Grecian ruins, ancient castles, and temples with the most incredible craftsmanship. None of it compared to the grainy black-and-white image of our child moving around. I can't wait to hold it.

He smiled. She included a photo, but it wasn't the same as getting to see their baby move.

His smile disappeared as he read further.

I wish you were here.

He looked down at the other letters stacked neatly inside. He'd missed out on so much. Even after everything, she had still wanted him in the baby's life. In her life. She'd forgiven him, extended him grace.

And really, had she reacted any differently than he had when she'd initially told him about her offer to Bridget? He'd been furious, and that had been with her confessing directly to him. How would he have felt if he had learned about her offer from someone else? Had felt like he was being lied to?

He'd made poor choices, largely out of fear, but

also pride. But those choices hadn't erased what they had together. From the beginning, there'd been something between them, something special that had been magnified in Glenvarra, away from the hustle of London.

And then he'd run away. Out of anger, pride, and above all, fear. And for what? To be separated from a woman who brought out the best in him? A woman he couldn't stop thinking about, whom he ached to hold?

He hit a button on his desk. "Jolene, my office, please."

A moment later Jolene, a middle-aged woman with a cloud of silvery hair and black-framed glasses, bustled in. "Yes, Mr. Sawyer?"

"I need to fly back to Dublin. Tomorrow."

Her eyes widened behind her glasses. "What about the meeting with—"

"Ned can handle it. I'd like my schedule cleared the rest of the week."

Jolene frowned. "Are you feeling okay, sir?"

"I am. I just need to get back to Dublin."

"All right." She started to turn, then stopped. "Oh, this came for you this morning."

He recognized the cursive on the envelope, nearly snatched it out of Jolene's hands, and ripped it open before she was even out the door. She cast a worried glance over her shoulder as she shut it.

He pulled the letter out and unfolded it. It was short, mostly about Mina's mother buying the baby an outfit and looking forward to her appointment next week. But toward the end, he saw it.

Wish you were here.

He traced his fingers over the words, over her name. Images flashed through his head like a movie: the first time he met her, the first time she stood up to him in a meeting, the night she came into his office. And then more recent memories paraded through, from seeing her on the cliffs to watching that incredible smile of hers when the falcon landed on her arm.

He'd loved being with her. Even after their falling-out, his desire for her had simmered below his persistent attempts to extinguish it. Because he loved her.

He loved her, and he was hundreds of miles away.

He buzzed Jolene again. "I've changed my mind," he said as she walked in. He'd already started moving about the office, collecting his things. "Get me there this afternoon."

"Sir, you can't—"

"I can, and I will, Jolene. I have to get back to Glenvarra and beg the woman I love to give me a second chance."

Mina

Mina stared out her kitchen window, a cup of tea in her hands. The baby was quieter today, as if sensing her mood. She felt a few nudges and kicks but not the usual rolling gymnastics, thank goodness. Normally she loved feeling the baby move. But today she was grateful for the respite.

The demolition of the North Wing weighed on her. She knew it was necessary, knew the ruins had become far too much of a risk for there to be any other course of action.

It would be like a death. A funeral for a magnificent structure that had withstood so much.

But then in the spring there would be new life. New construction to rebuild the North Wing, coupled with the silver lining of Bridget offering Mina a one-year heritage consultancy contract while preserving her current position. Once Bridget had assured Mina that she wasn't offering it to her out of guilt, Mina had accepted.

So much to appreciate. In time, she'd be able to focus on the blessings.

But right now, she missed Barrett. Missed him so much it hurt.

She'd gone through the motions at the banquet and managed to make it through to the end. Arlowe and Ivy had left around midnight. They both picked up that something was wrong and had offered to stay, but Mina had reassured them that she would tell them everything soon. She had just wanted to be alone.

Thankfully, she'd already requested the following week off to recuperate from the banquet. To stay home and sleep in, cry, or eat yet another tub of ice cream.

When her mother had knocked on her door the morning after the banquet to check on her, Mina had slowly pulled it open.

A leanbh, *are you sick?*

Mina had slowly shaken her head. *You were right. I got my heart broken.*

And then she'd collapsed into tears. Her mother had walked with her over to the couch, sat next to her, wrapped her arms around her, and rocked her back and forth.

The first two days had been the hardest. Aside from going outside to sit in the back garden, Mina hadn't left the house.

Mama had stopped by with gifts, including a fluffy white top and pants with a matching hat for the baby. Mina had managed to force a smile even though her thoughts had turned to Barrett. What would he think of the tiny clothes? Would he get the same look on his face as he had when he heard the baby's heartbeat?

On the third day she'd forced herself to go to a café and brought along a journal. She'd intended to write down her thoughts, make a list of the things she had to be grateful for. Instead, she'd written Barrett a letter. And this time she'd mailed it.

She didn't expect a reply. Not for a while anyway. Eventually Barrett would reach out about coparenting. She didn't doubt that. She wanted her child to have Barrett in its life.

A soft sigh escaped. She still wanted Barrett in her life, too. Her reaction had been unwarranted. If she had offered him the chance to explain, the same chance she wished he would have given her months ago, could they have had more?

It stung to realize how deeply her fears had taken root. She'd always chalked up that emptiness inside her to not knowing who her father was. But when she thought about it, it had been mostly curiosity with the occasional sadness in those early years. The ache had only started to grow after she'd overheard Mama and *Mamó*. After she'd learned that her father hadn't wanted her.

She'd never met him, yet she'd allowed him to wound her. Had spent so much of her life chalking up the pain to simply not knowing her past when in reality she had been avoiding the truth: she was afraid that she wasn't worth staying for. She'd kept boys mostly at a distance in secondary school, had used her studies as an excuse to not let her romantic relationships in university go too deep.

This time, because she had been prepared to fully surrender herself to a man she had finally admitted she was in love with, she had done exactly what Barrett had done to her in London. She'd lashed out first, chosen anger to avoid fear.

And lost him anyway.

A knock sounded on her door.

"Yes?"

The door swung open. "Just me, dear."

A moment later Ethna Callahan appeared in the doorway. She was twenty years older than her daughter but had been mistaken on more than one occasion as Mina's sister. With the same bright blue eyes and red-gold curls, the primary differences were the silver strands in her hair and the darker freckles dotted across her narrow face.

"How does potato and leek soup sound for dinner?" Mama asked as she set a brown paper bag on the counter.

Mina's fingers tightened around the mug. The same soup she and Barrett had shared at the taste testing for the banquet. Right before they'd walked out to the falconry and he'd taken the call that had changed everything. "Sounds nice," she forced out.

Mama sat beside her. "You miss him."

"I do. And I hurt him. I feel like I'm a failure. I did what you always warned me not to do and I fell for the wrong man." She paused, then slowly looked up at her mother, into a face that looked so much like her own. "Except he's not the wrong man. He's generous and he listens and he tries to be a better person, and I..." She shook her head. "I didn't realize how scared I've been all these years. And I let that fear take over and I pushed him away. He still wants to be there for the baby, but he…we…"

Mama reached out and grasped her hand. "I did you a great disservice."

"What?"

"I should have told you, Mina. About your father. I won't apologize for sheltering you in those early years. You deserved to have a childhood free of wondering why someone didn't want you. But when you asked that Father's Day, I should have told you. It was partly to protect you but also out of shame. Maybe if I had told you sooner, you would be able to trust easier."

"It's not your fault, Mama—"

"It is. I will tell you, though, that there are several things that signal that this is different. Your father left, but Barrett still wants to be involved And I heard from multiple people at the castle that he was kind." She gave Mina a wan smile. "I saw warning flags with your father long before I became pregnant with you. But I was so swept up in the romance and the luxury he offered me that summer that I ignored them. You didn't let yourself be carried away. Another good sign."

"We've hurt each other so much, though."

"Love isn't just happiness and butterflies. It's hard work, and there's still pain." Mama smiled. "You and I have certainly had our ups and downs."

"We have. But I didn't trust him, and he left."

Mama's face darkened. "And I don't like him

for that. But your situation is different than mine. He's different."

"I love him." Mina's voice cracked. "I was falling for him the whole time I was at Sawyer Development, and the night we spent together..." Her voice cracked again. "I'm sorry I hurt you. And I'm sorry I kept so much from you."

Mama reached out and stroked her hair. "No matter what happens between you and Barrett, you're going to be a fantastic mother."

"Well, I had a good example."

As her mother's eyes glistened, Mina's phone rang.

"Hello?"

"Mina? It's Bridget. I am so sorry, but is there any way you can come up tonight and do a brief dinner presentation? We have a high-profile guest staying in the Moon Spire Suite."

The most expensive suite. Bridget normally didn't roll out the red carpet to this extent, so this guest must be important.

"I'll pay you triple," Bridget added.

"You don't have to do that." Despite Bridget's protests, Mina knew she was feeling guilty. But she didn't want her to feel like she had to buy her way back into Mina's friendship.

"I'm calling you in while you're on leave. Of course I'm paying."

"All right. I can be there in an hour." She hung up.

"Are you seriously going into work?" Mama asked. "Aren't you on vacation for another few days?"

"It'll be a good distraction."

Mina hurriedly changed out of her casual wear and pulled on a pair of work pants and a loose top. She still hadn't gotten a new vehicle, so she borrowed her mother's and made the trek up to the castle.

Bridget had given no names for the mysterious guest staying in the Moon Spire Suite. But every now and then they would get a famous guest—a movie star or a politician. Maybe that was why Bridget was bending over backward for them.

She waved to the front desk attendant as she walked in, taking care not to look in the direction of the ballroom. The elevator ride to the top floor took less than fifteen seconds. She walked to the far end of the hallway and knocked on the door.

For a moment, there was nothing, and then a muffled "come in" sounded.

Mina twisted the knob, and the door swung open. It was a gorgeous suite with dark wood trim, crystal chandeliers, soaring ceilings, and arched windows that overlooked the cliffs, the country-side, and part of the North Wing.

"Hello?" She noted the table by the window with a candelabra and a bowl of red roses, along with the silver cart parked next to the table with covered dishes. "Hello?"

Mina's breath caught as Barrett stepped into view.

"Hello, Mina."

CHAPTER TWENTY-ONE

Barrett

HE WAS AN idiot. A complete and utter fool to think he could have walked away from Mina.

She stood just a few feet away, within reach but so far away. Her hair was pulled back into a loose braid, tendrils framing her face. Dressed in a relaxed silky top and dark pants, she looked every inch the professional.

But there were dark circles under her eyes. He had the same. The telltale sign of a broken heart.

"Barrett?"

His heart started to pound. He held up the envelope he had received that evening. "I got your letter."

She looked between him and the envelope, confusion and wariness written across her face. "So, you came here? To Glenvarra?"

"I was actually arranging a flight when my secretary brought your letter in."

Cautious hope flickered in her eyes. It kindled a similar feeling in his chest. "You were?"

"I was." He took a slow step toward her. "I told myself I was doing the right thing for both of us. That you would never be able to trust me, and that I would never be able to let myself believe in what we had. I told myself what we had was an illusion that couldn't hold up to reality." Another step.

She noticed but didn't back down.

"But I didn't even give it a chance," he went on. "As soon as I thought you were rejecting me, I pulled away."

"Barrett—"

"They were excuses. To help me put off acknowledging that I was in love with you."

Mina's hands flew to her mouth.

"I started falling for you the first day you started working for me. You smiled at me and I felt something inside my chest I hadn't felt before." He reached out, tentatively tucked a strand of hair behind her ear. "And that night, when I truly got to see you, have you all to myself, I fell in love."

Tears glinted in her eyes.

"I know it's a lot," he added softly, "especially after I left." He slid his hands up to cup her face. "I was a cruel coward, Sabrina. I cracked open my heart for the first time in years, and when I was faced with my first challenge, I faltered."

She wrapped her hands over his, leaned in to his touch. "I love it when you call me Sabrina."

"Do you?" He leaned down and brushed a gentle kiss over the tip of her nose. "No one else ever called you Sabrina, so I stopped."

"Don't stop," she murmured. "Don't ever stop."

"I'm in love with you, Sabrina."

"And I'm in love with you. I'm so sorry, Barrett. Right before Bridget told me about the North Wing and her phone call with you, I'd told Thomas I was retracting my proposal. That I wanted to give you and me a chance without adhering to some clause requiring we get married within a year."

Realization hit. "You were going to give up your inheritance."

"There was that possibility, yes."

Staggered by the enormity of what she was offering, Barrett let out a harsh breath. "Sabrina I'm—"

"How could you have known, Barrett?" Her voice broke. "I did the same thing. I jumped to conclusions. I didn't realize how much I've avoided trusting people over the years, specifically men. I didn't let myself get romantically involved because I was so scared of being abandoned the way my father abandoned my mother and me. I lived my life in so many ways, but I held myself back when it came to love.

"Until you. When I started falling in love with you, I worked so hard to keep my distance and keep the walls up between us. You said so many times you would never get married or have a family, and I was terrified of getting in too deep and having you not return my feelings. But then it seemed like maybe we had a chance, so I let myself hope."

"We both hoped."

"And we both hurt."

"We did," he agreed. "But I was told recently that loving someone often involves hurt."

Mina laughed quietly. "Have you been talking to my mother?"

"Bridget, actually."

"Well, my mother told me something similar. I won't promise that I won't hurt you again, Barrett, but I..." She swallowed hard. "I want to try again. If you'll have me."

"Do you trust me?"

She nodded without hesitation. "I do."

The honesty in her eyes staggered him. He captured her mouth with his, his heart swelling as she wrapped her arms around his neck. In that moment, he resolved to not let a single day go by without telling Mina how much he loved her.

Finally, he raised his head. "May I show you something?"

When she nodded again, he took her hand and led her out to the elevator. The food would stay warm until they got back. They rode the elevator down, and he led her out the doors first, taking her out to see the North Wing.

"I had my schedule cleared next week so I can be here with you."

Mina craned her head back to look at the North Wing. "Thank you."

"And I wanted to make one last memory before we say goodbye to it."

Mina turned just as he sank down onto one knee.

"Oh my God, Barrett."

He reached into his pocket and pulled out the small velvet box. "I wasn't sure I'd be able to find a ring in time because I told myself that no matter what, I was proposing to you today. But I stopped in town on my way up here, and when I saw this in the jeweler's window, I knew it had to be yours."

He flipped open the lid. A vintage silver ring nestled inside, carrying a large square-cut emerald surrounded by tiny diamonds.

"The jeweler said it was fashioned in the early 1900s. As soon as I saw it, I knew it was perfect for you. I know we'd talked about taking it slow before, but I don't want another day to go by without knowing you'll be my wife."

He took her hand in his.

"Sabrina Callahan, would you be my wife?"

"Yes." She nodded her head as tears streamed down her cheeks. "Yes, Barrett, I'll marry you."

He surged to his feet and swept her into his arms. "I'm never letting you go again," he vowed before he kissed her.

It was sometime later when Mina planted her hands on his chest and gently pushed him away. "But what about your job? Your company?"

"I'm looking to expand a little more. An office for Sawyer Development in Dublin."

Mina's eyes grew wide. "You would do that for me?"

"For you, my love, I would do anything."

"And you'll be happy here?"

"As long as I have you, Mina, I'll always be happy."

EPILOGUE

Barrett

Five years and two months later

"ALANNAH! HURRY UP, darling, we're going to be late." Mina shook her head as she walked toward Barrett. "I swear, that child takes more time picking out her clothes than I do."

Barrett grinned at her. "I don't mind."

Mina frowned. "Oh?"

"Gives us more time for this."

He wrapped an arm around her waist and pulled her close, silencing her shriek of surprise with a kiss. A moment later Mina moaned and sank into his arms. His hands pressed against her back as his body tightened. It had been over six years since he'd first met Mina, and he still wanted her just as much.

A sharp gasp had them springing apart.

"What are you doing?" Alannah demanded from the top of the stairs.

Barrett looked up and his breath caught. For a

moment all he could do was stare. Dressed in pink with a matching crown atop her red-gold curls, his daughter looked like a fairy princess.

His five-year-old fairy princess he could have sworn was a tiny baby just days ago.

"Daddy?"

The tentativeness in her voice had him taking the steps two at a time.

"You surprised me, that's all," he said as he knelt in front of her. "All grown up."

"I am five now," Alannah replied solemnly.

How had it already been five years since he and Mina had exchanged their vows in the courtyard of the castle?

So much had happened in those five years. He and Mina had bought a house just outside Glenvarra, minutes away from her mother and Róisín. Sawyer Development continued to thrive, including the office he opened in Dublin a few months after Alannah's birth. Mina had received her inheritance and set up a trust for renovating old buildings to be used for small businesses. The North Wing had been rebuilt in two years and opened with great fanfare.

And now…now he was getting ready to celebrate his daughter's fifth birthday.

"You look absolutely beautiful."

A slow grin spread across Alannah's face. "Really?" She dropped her voice to a whisper. "Am I as beautiful as Mommy?"

"What I love about both my girls," he said with a gentle tug on one of her curls, "is that you're both the most beautiful to me." His throat tightened. He wasn't going to cry. Not now. "Ready to go to your party?"

At her eager nod, he swooped her up into his arms and walked back down the stairs where Mina was waiting.

"Can I order any dessert?" Alannah asked as Mina draped a scarf around her small shoulders.

"Yes."

"How many desserts?"

"One," Mina said with a smile.

"But I'm five. Shouldn't I get five?"

Barrett laughed. "Nice try." He glanced at his watch. "We better hurry. You've got a crowd of people waiting."

"Really?" Alannah scampered towards the door. "Is Aunt Ivy there?"

"Yes, and Uncle Thomas and Aunt Deidre, Aunt Arlowe and Uncle Hart, *Mamó*, and half a dozen others. Don't forget your coat!" Mina chuckled as Alannah did a quick turnaround and grabbed her coat off the door handle. "She's been waiting for this since she was three."

"I like it, though." Barrett pulled her close again and kissed her forehead. "A family tradition. Dinner and dessert at Róisín on your fifth birthday. Although," he added as they walked toward the door, "I'm going to have a glass of brandy with my cake instead of milk."

"Hmm. I'd like to have a glass of wine, but that's going to have to wait awhile."

"Why is…" Barrett's voice trailed off. Excitement filled him. "Are you?"

Mina nodded, her eyes glassy. "I took the test this morning."

"Mina." He cupped her face in his hands, too overcome to say anything other than her name over and over.

"Are you okay, Daddy?"

He turned to see Alannah standing in the middle of the hallway, her jacket half-zipped and her crown cockeyed as she stared at them with suspicious eyes.

"I am. I'm just happy." He held out one arm. "Come here, birthday girl."

Alannah ran forward and threw her arms around his legs. Barrett pulled her and Mina close, savored the moment with his family of three even as he let himself imagine what life would look like this time next year with a new son or daughter added to the mix.

Mina cradled her head in the curve of his shoulder.

"Still happy," he murmured into her hair.

Her lips curved into a smile. "Still happy."

* * * * *

Look out for the next story in
How to Inherit a Fortune trilogy

Coming soon!

And if you enjoyed this story, check out these other great reads from Scarlett Clarke:

Snowbound Nights with Her Best Friend
The Billionaire She Loves to Hate
Royally Forbidden to the Boss

All available now!